Wishing

I heard my dad and my brother, Josh, talking in Josh's room. I stopped and listened to them. Josh was telling my dad about something that had happened in his gym class, and my dad was actually laughing about it. I listened awhile, but I felt like an intruder so I stayed outside the door.

Finally I went to my room. I was wishing things could have been different. I wanted the three of us to get along, but my father didn't seem to treat me the same when Josh was around.

**Other Apple Paperbacks
you will enjoy:**

Amanda the Cut-up
    by Vivian Schurfranz
Eat Your Heart Out, Victoria Chubb
    by Joyce Hunt
Kate's Book
    by Mary Francis Shura
My Sister, the Meanie
    by Candice F. Ransom

Living With Dad

Lynn Z. Helm

AN
APPLE
PAPERBACK

SCHOLASTIC INC.
New York Toronto London Auckland Sydney

ISBN 0-590-43011-4

Text copyright © 1990 by Lynn Zednick.
Illustrations copyright © 1990.

12 11 10 9 8 7 6 5 4   9/9 0 1 2 3/0

Printed in the U.S.A.   40
First Scholastic printing, June 1990

*For my mother and dad
who were the models for "Grandma and Grandpa"
and the best parents in the world.
Thanks for believing in me.*

1

I sat on my patchwork quilt bedspread and pulled on the little tufts of yarn that Grandma had left sticking out at the corners. I could hear the voices in the next room.

I slid one of the smooth strings between my fingers. I had been pulling on this yarn ever since I could remember. I guess it was kind of soothing. On hot summer days, I liked to lay on the cool material and pull the yarn through my fingers. I guess I did it mostly when I was upset or had something I needed to think over. It sounds silly, but it made me feel better. And today, I needed to feel a whole lot better.

My brother Josh and I were going to have to leave Grandma and Grandpa's farm and move to Dallas with our dad. I guess that wouldn't be so bad for the average kid, but Josh and I didn't even *remember* our dad. Heck, like my grandpa always says, "I wouldn't know him if he plowed me down with his tractor." (He wouldn't say that about my dad, of course. He would say that when someone would ask him if he knew so-and-so and my grandpa didn't know him.)

See, my mom and dad got a divorce when Josh and I were really little. My dad worked with an oil company in South America. He stayed there, and we moved to Grandma and Grandpa's farm. That was eight years ago. Then our mom died last year. I laid in my room and pulled on my quilt a lot for a while after she died. And just when things were finally starting to get better, we get this phone call from my dad saying he's coming home and he wants us to live with him.

I could hear my grandma's voice on the other side of the wall. "I wonder how long this will last. Children are a lot of work. He hasn't got any idea what it takes to raise a child."

My door opened, and Josh came in. He sat down at the foot of my bed. I usually like having Joshua around when I'm scared, but today he didn't look much better than I felt.

"Can you hear what they're saying?" he whispered.

I nodded. He moved back on the bed and put his ear to the wall. We could hear Grandpa saying, "Gracie, there's nothing we can do about it. After all, he *is* their father."

"Then where has he been all these years? Was he here when they had chicken pox? Did he see

2

them in the Thanksgiving Day parade the year their float won first place? Did he ever do any more than just send them expensive presents from all over the world?"

"Well, no matter what he's done in the past, he wants to make it up to them now."

"How? By waltzing in here and yanking those children out of the only home they've ever known? Taking them away from the people who love them?"

"He isn't taking them to China, Gracie. It's only Dallas. Only a few hours down the road. We can see them on weekends."

I don't know about Grandma, but it sure made *me* feel a lot better to know we would be just a few hours down the road. I closed my eyes and imagined Grandpa putting his arm around Grandma and squeezing her shoulders like he always did when she got upset.

I loved my grandma and grandpa more than anyone in the whole world. Except maybe Josh, of course. I was going to miss them so much.

Just thinking about leaving them behind made me get that sick feeling you get just before your eyes fill up with water, and you know you're fixing to cry. I reached over and grabbed Harold. (He's this old bear I've had since forever.) I squeezed my eyes real tight, but tears still leaked out and plopped right onto Harold's head.

I heard Josh slide over next to me and felt his arm go around my shoulders. "It's going to be all right," he whispered. "You just wait and see."

I looked at his face. He didn't look so scared anymore. "Is it really going to be all right?"

He nodded. "You bet. If we stick together, we'll be okay. And if we don't like it there, we'll just get on a bus and come on home."

"Yeah," I said, feeling better than I had all morning. "Yeah, we'll just get on a bus and come on home." I laid my head against Josh and listened to the voices in the living room.

"It may not be that far," Grandma was saying, "but it's a whole new world to those children. They've never been in a city. I haven't been to Dallas since they shot President Kennedy. Now, what kind of a city would let that happen, I ask you? Nothing but murderers and weirdos in Dallas. That's what I think."

"Oh, now surely there are a few good people in Dallas, Grace."

"Humph," was all she said.

I turned to Josh. It felt like my eyes were popping out of my head. "Do you really think Dallas is full of murderers and weirdos?"

"Naw. How would Gram know? You really want to trust the judgment of somebody who's never left Wildflower?" I smiled at him. Josh was so smart.

4

I wiped my nose with the back of my hand, even though I knew better. Grandma says a lady always uses a tissue. But Grandma was in the next room.

A little while later, I was in the living room when my father's dark blue car pulled into the gravel driveway. I heard the wheels crunching on the road, and I went to the window. He got out of his car and stretched. He was so tall. I didn't think he would be so tall.

I peeked at him through the slit in Grandma's lace curtains. Joshua saw what I was doing. "Stop that, Robbie. It's not polite." I let the curtain drop, but I could still see him through the filmy fabric. He wasn't bad-looking, but I would have liked him more if he'd been someone else's dad coming to take them to Dallas and not me.

As he got closer to the porch, I saw he looked a lot like Joshua. The same olive skin and dark curly hair. My hair was curly, too, but not quite that dark. I touched one of the long strands of curls and wondered if I looked anything like my dad.

The doorbell rang, and I jumped away from the window. I knew Grandma was on her way into the room, and she wouldn't like my spying on him. Her long hair was in a bun. Wispy little pieces had fallen out and were flying in her face, tickling

5

her. Grandma scrunched up her nose and fanned at the irritating hairs before she opened the door.

"Come in, Willis," Grandma said. You could tell by the voice she used that Grandma wasn't very happy to see him. "Children, go get your things."

I just stood there by the window staring at him. Joshua nudged my arm. I followed him out of the room and into my bedroom to get my suitcase.

We came back, and my father was still standing in the doorway where we'd left him. He had a sort of pained expression on his face, like a guy who'd wandered into the wrong house. For an instant I hoped maybe he had made a mistake and he wasn't our father at all. Then I looked at my brother and back at my dad, and I knew that there was no mistake about it. This man was our dad, all right.

Grandpa came into the room and put his arm around Grandma. With his other arm he stretched a hand out toward our father. "How are you, Willis? It's been a long time."

"Yes, sir, it certainly has." They shook hands.

"These here are your children, Robin and Joshua. Children, you remember your daddy."

He rubbed his hands together and had this goofy grin on his face. "Well, we'd better get started." He reached out and took the two big suitcases. Josh and I picked up the overnight bags. "Is this it?" he asked.

6

"For now," Grandma said. "We'll send the other things along later." I hadn't wanted her to send the things at all. I wanted to leave them at Grandma's house so I could come back here later on, and they would be waiting for me.

I turned to my grandma. I was trying very hard not to cry. Joshua told me to be brave because Grandma was old and it was hard for her to say good-bye to us. I didn't think it had anything to do with being old, though. 'Cause I was only eleven and it wasn't easy for me to say good-bye, either.

Grandma reached out and wrapped me in her arms, and I couldn't help myself. I started to cry. I knew she was crying, too. That made me cry harder.

I let go of Grandma and grabbed Grandpa. He squeezed me so hard I could hardly breathe. When he let go, I backed away just in time to see Josh brush a tear from his cheek. In fact, the only one not crying on that old porch that morning was my father.

"Hey, now, it's not all that bad," my father said. "You can come back and visit sometimes."

"Your dad's right," Grandpa said. "You can come and see us and tell us all about your new home."

"We will," I promised. I reached down and

picked up my overnight bag again. In my other hand, I had Harold. My father put the suitcases in the trunk. He offered to take my overnight case, too, but I had some of Grandma's chocolate chip cookies inside, and I told him I wanted to keep it in the car with me. He opened the door to the backseat so I could get in. He noticed Harold under my arm.

"Looks like you've had him for quite a while. Tell you what," he said. "When we get to Dallas, I'll take you down to Neiman Marcus and you can pick out a brand-new bear."

"I don't want a new bear," I said, climbing into the backseat. I turned around and got up on my knees so I could see out the back window. Grandma and Grandpa were still standing on the porch. Grandpa had his arm around Grandma, and it almost looked like he was holding her up. I bet she was crying. I squeezed Harold tighter and wished like anything it was Grandma I was holding onto.

The car lurched forward. I kept looking out the back window through the cloud of dust. I didn't want to forget a single thing about that moment. I wanted to memorize every detail about Grandma and Grandpa's farm so I could call it up again when I got to missing them really bad.

That was my home back there, and I was leaving it behind. I didn't care if the man in the front seat was my father or not. It wasn't fair to make us leave like that. He might have been taking us to live in some fancy house in Dallas, but that old farmhouse getting smaller and smaller in the distance was the only place I'd ever want to live.

2

As we got closer to Dallas the tall buildings of the big city seemed to shoot up out of the flat ground. One building looked like a giant ice-cream cone or maybe a stick with a golf ball on the top of it.

"Wow, look at that!" Josh exclaimed, pointing to the funny-looking building off in the distance.

"That's Reunion Tower," Dad said. "There's a restaurant up there. That big ball turns around all night long and you can see the whole city while you eat dinner."

"No kidding!" Josh said. "Can we eat up there sometime?"

"Sure," Dad replied. He looked into the rear-view mirror. "How about that, Robin? Would you like to go up there for dinner one of these nights?"

I shrugged. "I guess so. Do they have fried chicken?"

"Well, I don't know. I've never ordered fried chicken there, but I'm sure they have it."

"I bet it's not as good as Grandma's," I mumbled, and then I scrunched down in the seat and hugged Harold tighter.

There were twisting highways with cars whizzing by all around us. I'd never seen so many cars in one place before. In spite of myself, I couldn't help looking out my window. But at least I wasn't as bad as Josh. He kept "wow-ing" this and "geezing" that. You'd think we'd never been to a city before, but we had. We'd been to Lubbock with Grandma and Grandpa.

We drove into a neighborhood of really pretty brick houses with great big yards and huge trees that were dancing in the wind. My father pulled the car into a circular driveway and stopped. "Well, this is it."

"Wow," Josh gasped. "Are we going to live here?"

I looked at the fancy glass-and-wooden door and the neat little flowers all tucked safely behind some kind of green metal border. I thought about Grandma's lace curtains on the window of the farmhouse and the spindly blades of grass that kept poking up in Grandma's rosebushes, and decided I still liked Grandma's house better.

I was trying to get the dumb seat belt undone. My father opened the door and leaned in. "You need a hand?"

"I can get it."

He shrugged. "If you're sure." He left the door open and went around to get our suitcases out of the trunk. He stopped on the porch and looked back at me. I quickly looked down at the seat belt. I saw a little red button and pressed on it. The seat belt popped off. He followed Josh into the house, leaving the front door open.

I stepped into the house. The floor in the hallway was white tile. It looked like you could almost see the whole house from the front door. It was pretty big for just my father. There was a living room right in front of me and a dining room on one side and a hallway on the other. Above the living room was a second floor that had a railing along the hall so you could look down on the people in the living room below. Didn't make much sense to me to put a second story on top of a house if you were only going to put it on half the house.

Josh came flying out of one of the rooms above and leaned on the railing. "Come on up, Robbie. Wait'll you see it!" Can you believe that? This morning, Josh and I were going to run away from this place and go back to our grandparents', and now he was acting like he didn't remember we had a grandma and grandpa.

"Come on up, sweetie," Dad said, appearing on the landing next to Josh. "I'll show you your room."

12

I carried my overnight bag and Harold up the stairs to where they were waiting. Both of them had the same goofy smile on their faces. It was funny you could look so much like somebody you didn't even know.

My room was lots bigger than the one I'd had at Grandma's. There was a pink bedspread with ruffles around the bottom and matching curtains on the window. The wallpaper even matched.

"I hope you like the decorating. I didn't know what to put in a girl's room. I had the decorator do this one herself. If you don't like it, we can start all over."

"It's very nice," I said as politely as I could. I set my overnight bag on the floor next to my suitcase.

"This is the bathroom," he said, opening a door I thought might be another closet. "Josh's room is on the other side."

"You ought to see it, Rob, it's got the neatest bunk beds. They're built right into the wall. It has a desk and everything."

My dad smiled and ruffled Josh's hair. "Well, I'll let you two get unpacked and settled in," he said. "Come on downstairs when you finish, and we'll decide what we're going to do tonight."

"Hey, come on in and check out my room," Josh said with excitement. I followed him through the big bathroom into his room. It was pretty nice. It was even bigger than my room.

"Is that bathroom just for us?" I whispered. It was enormous. Especially just for two people.

"I guess so. Dad's room is downstairs. I think I saw a bathroom by the kitchen. That must be his."

At the farm, we had just one bathroom. Grandpa had put it in when they bought the old farmhouse because the bathroom had been outside before that.

I went back to my room. I dragged my suitcase up on the bed and took out my clothes. I hardly had enough to fill even a portion of the huge closet. I took my empty suitcases and put them on the floor of the closet.

I went back and sat down on the bed. I ran my hand across the crisp, shiny bedspread. It felt new and stiff. I wanted my old quilt that Grandma had made. At least it would have made this room feel a little bit like mine.

I put Harold between the pillows. "Now, I know this doesn't feel like home, Harold, but you don't have to be scared. We're going to stay here for a while. If we don't like it, we'll just go on back to Grandpa and Grandma's." I patted him on the head. That always made him feel better.

I took my comb, brush, and mirror over to the

dresser and laid them out neatly like Grandma always did on her dresser. She had given me the silver vanity set for my birthday last year. I could almost hear her voice saying, "Every young lady needs a vanity set." It had seemed like a dumb present at the time. I lightly traced the bumpy surface of the flowers on the back of the mirror and thought it was the most beautiful present anyone had ever given me.

Josh banged on my door, and I just about jumped out of my skin. "You coming?"

I followed him down the stairs through the kitchen and into what looked like another living room. Dad was watching a baseball game. "Who's playing?" Josh asked as he sat down beside our dad.

"The Rangers and the Angels." He looked over at Josh. "Do you like baseball?"

"You bet," Josh said.

"I can see about getting tickets to next week's game. Would you like that?"

"Wow," was all he said. For a thirteen-year-old, my brother had some vocabulary.

After the ball game, we decided we would go to Reunion Tower for dinner and take a tour of the city.

I went up to my room to get dressed. I put on the jumper Grandma had made me for the first day of school last year. It was already getting too small. Maybe I really was starting to grow, just like Grandma said I would.

I went into the bathroom and looked at myself in the mirror. I was sorry the jumper was getting too small. I rubbed my hand over the smooth blue corduroy. There were little pink flowers in the material, and Grandma had made me a pink blouse the very same color. But the best thing about it was, she had let me pick out the material and the pattern all by myself.

When I got downstairs, Josh and my dad were waiting for me. My dad was wearing a shirt and tie like he was going to church. He looked at my jumper. "Is that what you're going to wear?"

"Grandma made it," I said proudly.

"Well, don't worry about it tonight. I'll have Mrs. Nelson take you shopping next week, and we'll get you some decent clothes."

"Who's Mrs. Nelson?" Josh asked.

"My housekeeper. She'll be here when I'm at work," he said as we started out the door.

Decent clothes? I looked down at the jumper Grandma had made me. What did *that* mean? What was wrong with my jumper except it was getting too small? I remembered when Grandma had me try it on the night before school started last year. I came into the living room, and Grandpa put his paper down and whistled at me.

16

My face got red and Grandpa said, "It won't be long before we're fighting those boys off with a stick, Mama." Grandma smiled, and you could see she was real proud.

I got in the backseat. I wished we were going back to the farm for Grandma's cooking instead of to a fancy restaurant sitting on top of a giant stick in the sky.

3

Somehow we made it through the weekend. It was the longest one of my life. It felt like it lasted a month. Josh didn't seem to mind, though. It was hard to figure him out. When Grandma and Grandpa got that first phone call from my dad, saying he was moving to Dallas and he wanted us to live with him, Josh was more upset than me. He kept saying maybe it wouldn't be so bad if we just stuck together. But so far, it looked like the person he was doing most of the sticking to was my dad.

I walked into the kitchen Monday morning and saw the refrigerator door was open. Sticking out from the refrigerator door was a rather large behind that I knew didn't belong to Josh or to my dad. A loud sigh came from behind the door, and one of the tallest ladies I've ever seen in my life stood up and blew a puff of hair off her face.

She saw me standing there, and her face

erupted into a great big smile. "Well, you must be Robin."

"Yes, ma'am."

"Oh, now, don't you 'yes, ma'am,' me. I'm Mrs. Nelson." She stepped away from the refrigerator and gave the door a shove with her hip that sent it slamming shut. "I'm just about to make some breakfast. Do you like French toast?"

"Yes, ma'am. I mean, Mrs. Nelson."

"That's still a big mouthful for such a little girl. Why don't you call me Hattie?" I nodded. "I swear you are just a little bitty slip of a girl. Now how old did your daddy tell me you are?"

"Eleven, but I'll be twelve on my next birthday."

Hattie exploded into laughter that made her big body shake all over. She slapped her leg and surprised me with an enormous hug. "That's real good, sweetheart. Twelve usually does follow eleven."

She let go of me and started pulling utensils out of the cupboards. "Can I help?" I asked.

"You sure can. You can sit right up here." She whisked me into the air like I was a feather pillow Grandma kept on her bed back home, and plopped me down on a cabinet. "Now, your job is to supervise. Don't let me screw up."

"But I don't know anything about French toast."

"You know how to eat it, don't you?"

"Yes," I nodded.

"Well, that's enough."

Hattie got to work making the French toast. She mixed eggs and milk and spices in a blender and then poured the mixture into a plate. She took the bread and dipped it quickly into the mixture and slapped it onto the hot griddle. My dad had this really neat thing right in the middle of the stove. It was a grill and a griddle already built in. I thought about how much easier it would be for Grandma to make bacon and eggs on Sunday morning if she had a stove like that.

"Hey, what's going on in here?" Dad asked from the kitchen door. He was buttoning the cuffs on his shirt. I always did that for Grandpa on Sundays before we went to church. Grandma used to do it, but sometimes her arthritis was too bad and she couldn't do it, so it had become my job.

"We're getting breakfast, Mr. W."

Dad came over and lifted me off the cabinet as quickly as Hattie had lifted me up. "Let's try to break any bad habits the children may have, Mrs. Nelson, all right?"

"Bad habits?" I asked.

"I'd rather you sit on the *chairs* in the kitchen. Cabinets are for food. Chairs are for little people." He smiled at me.

"But I . . ."

"I put her up there, sir. It won't happen again."

"Good," he said. With that he left the kitchen, still trying to button the sleeve of his shirt.

"At least not while you're home," Hattie said, winking at me.

She handed me a plate of hot French toast. "Here now, go gob that full of syrup and butter and put a little meat on those bones."

My father came back into the kitchen with the morning paper. Both of his sleeves were buttoned. "I'll have your breakfast in a jiffy," Hattie said.

"Just coffee for me."

"Now, sir, how can you expect to make it through a busy day on an empty stomach."

"I said 'No, thank you,' Mrs. Nelson. Coffee will be fine."

Hattie got this funny look on her face. "Yes, sir. Coffee."

I ate my French toast and looked at the back of the newspaper my father was holding in front of his face. Living with Dad was turning out a lot worse than I had thought it might. So far the only good part about this whole thing was Hattie, and I didn't think my father liked her very much.

Josh came into the kitchen wearing just his pajama bottoms. "Hey, there, young man, I bet you're Josh. Sit down. I just happen to have an extra plate of French toast," Hattie said, setting the French toast down in front of Josh. "I'm Hattie."

The paper came down, and my father looked out at us across the table. "But you will call her Mrs. Nelson."

"Aw, I don't mind if the kids call me Hattie."

"Mrs. Nelson, please. I'd like the children to learn respect for their elders. Calling you by your first name may not bother *you*, but that kind of familiarity could seem fresh to others. Let's just make it easy all the way around, shall we?"

"What's an elder?" I asked. I thought it had something to do with the men who collected the money at church. But Hattie wasn't a man, and we weren't at church.

"An adult, honey. Now eat your breakfast." He disappeared behind his paper again.

"This is great," Josh said enthusiastically.

"Would you like some more? There's plenty." I think it made Hattie happy when you liked her cooking.

"You bet," Josh replied.

Hattie reached over and took my plate. "How about you, peanut; you want some more, too?"

"Yes, please, Hattie. Uh . . . Mrs. Nelson."

The paper came down again. "Since we've got a month before school starts, I thought you kids might like to take some lessons at the club."

"What club?" Josh asked.

"Twin Lakes Country Club. The clubhouse isn't far from here. You could ride your bikes over there while I'm at work."

"But we don't have any bikes," I said.

"Oh, I must have forgotten that part. Mrs. Nelson, do you think that French toast could wait a minute while we take a look in the garage?" my father asked.

"I'll keep it warm," she said. The way her eyes were smiling, I figured she knew what was in the garage. Josh and I jumped up from the table to see for ourselves. There were two brand-new bikes. Josh's was great. It was a red one that looked like a ten-speed. It was easy to tell which one he'd bought for me. Not only was it a girl's bike, but it had a white basket on the front of it. It was a lot smaller than Josh's, too. But at least it was a bike.

"As soon as you get dressed, you can try them out." He looked at me. "Do you know how to ride a bike, Robin?"

"Of course, she does," Josh said defensively. "She's been riding my bike since she was five years old."

"Oh. Well, maybe you need a bigger bike, then."

My face lit up. "That would be great."

"Okay, tell you what I'll do. When I get home tonight we'll take this back to the store, and you can pick out any bike you like. How's that?"

"That's terrific!" My father looked really happy when he left for work. I know I was happy for the first time since I'd left Grandpa and Grandma's.

I came into the kitchen. Mrs. Nelson was cleaning up the breakfast dishes. "Can I help?" I asked.

"No. This is what I get paid for. You just run along and play."

I went back into the living room. I looked around my father's house. There really wasn't anything to play with. It was full of antiques and art from all over the world. The furniture didn't even look comfortable. I went over to a carved wooden chair and sat down just to make sure. It was hard and cold.

Up in my room, I told Harold all about Mrs. Nelson. I promised him I'd introduce him later. He liked that idea. I don't think Harold liked my dad very well. He wasn't happy about being there, either. But I told him he'd feel a lot better after he got to know Mrs. Nelson.

Later, I took Harold out on the grass to read a book. Josh had ridden off on his bike somewhere. I would be happy when Dad exchanged my bike, and I could go with Josh. I didn't blame him for wanting to ride his new bike; I just wished we both could have gone.

Mrs. Nelson opened the heavy front door and

came outside. She pushed the back of her hand across her forehead and wiped the sweat away. "Whew. It's hot out here, peanut. How can you stand it?"

"I dunno. Mrs. Nelson, do you know when my dad will be home?"

"Well, he generally gets home around six-thirty or seven o'clock. And that's another thing: Let's just say you call me Hattie when it's just the two of us."

"But my dad said — "

"Well, you never mind that. It'll be our little secret. Just between friends." She winked at me. "What d'ya say? We got a deal?" She stretched her hand out to me.

I nodded. "We got a deal." I shook her big, warm hand.

Her arm wrapped around me, and we started toward the house. "Then let's go on in and see what we've got for lunch, peanut. What do you say about that?"

"Oh, I almost forgot. Can Harold come, too?"

"Who's Harold?"

I pulled away from her and ran back to get him. "This is Harold." I held him up for her to see.

"Why, aren't you handsome, Harold." She shook his paw. "I'm happy to meet you, sir."

Harold liked Hattie. I knew he would.

* * *

I spent most of the afternoon following Hattie around the house. Josh had met some boy on the bike trail and they went off to ride bikes all afternoon. I wasn't used to that. On the farm, we were pretty much the only kids around, and we did almost everything together. I couldn't wait till tomorrow when I would have a bike, too.

Hattie let me set the table for dinner. She showed me how to put the silverware on and fold the napkins. I was the official taste-tester and bowl-licker. I checked everything before Hattie put it on the table. She said that could be my job. I liked that job. Especially the bowl-licking part. She made German chocolate cake for dessert, and I got to lick the bowl. Boy, would Josh be mad if he knew about that.

Josh came in just as Hattie was putting the frosting on the cake. He slammed through the back door and ran into the bathroom. He came out with his hair all stuck down to his forehead.

"Hot out there?" Hattie asked.

"Yeah."

"Have some lemonade," Hattie said. She poured him a big glass of lemonade with lots of ice. It was easy to get ice at my dad's house. He had a door right on the refrigerator that dropped ice out when you pushed the lever.

"I think I'm going to like it here," Josh said, just as the phone rang.

Hattie answered it. I heard her say, "Of course, it's no problem. I'll just go ahead and feed the children. Don't you worry about a thing, sir."

She hung up the phone. "That was your father. He's involved in some meeting. Says he won't be home until late. He wants you kids to go ahead and eat without him."

"But what about my bike?" I asked. I felt tears stinging in my eyes. "If he doesn't get home until the stores are closed, we can't take it back."

Hattie sat down and pulled me onto her lap. "Well, maybe you and I will take that old bike back in the morning. What do you say about that?"

I nodded and swallowed my tears. I didn't want Hattie to think I was a big baby. I got off her lap and went around to my chair. I picked at my dinner and went right upstairs after I ate. I told Harold my dad wouldn't be home until later. And then I cried. It was okay, though. Harold didn't mind.

4

I wasn't asleep when the light came under the door. But as soon as I heard the doorknob turning, I shut my eyes real fast and pretended I was. Someone was standing there. I barely peeked out from under my eyelashes, and I saw my dad. I shut my eyes again and rolled toward the wall trying to look like I was asleep. He stood there a long time. Then finally he closed the door and went away.

I rolled onto my back. The shadows from the big tree outside my window danced on the ceiling. Watching the shadow reminded me of Grandpa and Grandma's. Back home, I loved to open the window just when it was turning springtime and smell the new leaves on the trees. A cool breeze would wash over me, and it was almost like sleeping outside. I went to my window and sat on the window seat. Would it smell the same here next spring?

The sun felt warm and bright when I opened

my eyes. I was still on the window seat. My neck was stiff from sleeping sitting up. I stood up and stretched. It was another sunny day. A perfect day for a bike ride. If I had a bike, that is.

Hattie was in the kitchen alone clanging dishes around and making lots of noise. "Hey there, peanut, how does bacon and eggs sound?"

"Okay." I went over and leaned on the cabinet to watch what she was doing. She cracked eggs just like Grandma. With one hand.

"You like them scrambled?"

"Sure. You want me to set the table?"

"If you want to. That'd be nice." She reached up and took plates and glasses out of the cabinet. I started putting them on the table.

"Good morning, good morning." My dad came into the kitchen carrying his newspaper under his arm. His sleeve was flapping, and he set the paper on the table so he could button it. "Everybody sleep all right?" he asked, struggling to button his sleeve.

"Yes, sir," I said. I set the plates down on the table. "I could do that for you."

"That would be great." He stuck his arm out, and I buttoned his sleeve.

"You sure make that look easy," he said, shaking his head in amazement. "I always have the worst time with these darned things. I tried cuff links once. That was even worse." He picked up the paper and sat down at the table. "Thanks, sweetie."

I began folding napkins and putting them next to the plates.

"I came in to say good night when I got home, but you were dead to the world. I didn't want to wake you. Listen, I'm sorry about that bike business."

"It's okay." At least he remembered. It wasn't like he forgot all about me.

He put his hand over the top of mine and squeezed. "Listen, I'll get away a little early today and we'll take care of it this afternoon. How would that be?"

"There's no need for you to get off early, Mr. W. I could take her."

"They owe me a little time off. We'll do it this afternoon. Tell you what you *can* do, though," he said folding his paper back and snapping it noisily. "You can take Robin and Josh shopping for some decent clothes."

"I have decent clothes," I said.

"Well, honey, they may have been all right for the farm, but you're in the city now. You're going to be starting school in a few weeks. Don't you want to look like the other girls?"

"I guess," I mumbled.

"That's what I thought," he said. And then he

smiled at me. "Besides, I bet you'd much rather go shopping for new clothes than ride a bike around in the heat." I was going to tell him I'd much rather go on a bike ride with Josh, but my dad had already disappeared behind his newspaper again.

After the breakfast dishes were all done, Hattie got her purse and came into the family room to get Josh and me.

"Aw, gee, do I have to go?" Josh said. "I already told Nick I'd come over this morning. He's going to show me a pond where there's a bunch of frogs and water snakes."

"Well, he can show you after lunch because your father wants you to have some new clothes. Come on." She went over and turned the TV off. "The sooner we get a move on, the quicker you can get back here."

"Aw, Hattie," he said as he followed us out to her car.

The mall was the biggest place I'd ever seen. Hattie called it "The Galleria." It was three stories high and had so many stores you couldn't begin to go to all of them. There was a glass dome on the roof, and Hattie said they even had a jogging track up there.

I stayed real close to Hattie and kept watching

for the weirdos and murderers Grandma said lived in Dallas, but mostly I just saw a lot of ordinary-looking people.

I guess it was actually kind of fun picking out a whole bunch of new clothes all at once. I wasn't sure when I was going to wear them all, though.

Josh wasn't having as much fun as I was. He kept dancing around the children's department asking how much longer we were going to be. It hadn't taken him as long to find things. He just grabbed stuff and said, "Yeah, I like this and this and this." He didn't even want to try anything on. Hattie was making me try everything on.

We finally left the store with loads of shopping bags. "How would you children like to have lunch here?" Hattie said.

"I saw a McDonald's on the second floor," Josh said.

"Well, there are nice restaurants all along here," Hattie pointed out.

"But we like McDonald's," I said. "And Grandma and Grandpa don't ever let us eat there."

"McDonald's it is!" Hattie said. Then she looked at Josh. "Lead the way, young man."

When we came home from the mall, I was surprised to see my dad's car in the driveway. He was in the family room with papers spread out all over the desk in front of him. He stood up when we came in and took some of the packages from Hattie.

"Well, Mrs. Nelson, how did it go?"

"Wonderfully, sir. We found several things. I'll leave the sales tags on them so you can return anything you don't like."

"If Robin and Josh like them, I'm sure I will, too." I thought about my blue jumper and wasn't so sure about that.

"Hey, how about putting those things away so we can go see my surprise?" Dad asked.

"Surprise!" Josh yelled. "Hurry up, Robbie, let's go. Come on, I'll race you."

"Okay," I said running for the door, "but I get a head start."

"Hey, you two," my father yelled. We both skidded to a stop. "No running in the house."

I thought Dad's surprise might be that we were going to get my new bike, but I didn't see the other one in the trunk to be returned. "Where are we going?" I asked.

"You'll see." I settled into the backseat and listened to my father give us a tour of the neighborhood. He turned into a big driveway and drove up to a huge brick building with tall windows. It looked almost like a great big house. I slid forward on the seat.

"Where are we?" I asked.

"The club. We're going to sign up for tennis lessons."

"Both of us?" I asked. I'd always wanted to try tennis. At school we played badminton sometimes, and I was pretty good. The gym teacher said I had good hand-eye coordination, whatever that meant.

I followed them into the clubhouse. People seemed to know my dad. He introduced us to some of them as we went through. We followed him into a store filled with all kinds of sports equipment. Dad said it was called the pro shop.

"Jeff," Dad said to the man behind the counter, "I want you to meet my children." The man came over to us. "I'm interested in signing them up for tennis lessons. Have you got any openings?"

"For you, Mr. Welborn, you bet."

Jeff looked like a tennis player. He had on white shorts and a white shirt. He was also very tan and very cute. I was even more excited about the tennis lessons.

"Have either of you ever played tennis before?" Jeff asked. We both shook our heads. "Then I'll start you out together with the basics."

"Do you think that'll work?" Dad asked.

"What do you mean?"

"Well, do you think Robin can keep up with her brother? If he's anything like me, he'll probably

34

catch on pretty quick. And if Robin's like her mother, she may have trouble returning the ball." He smiled down at me and messed up my hair. I'm surprised he didn't burn his hand with the steam coming out of my head.

I had news for him. He wasn't the only one in the family who was athletic. I was one of the first ones picked for anything when we chose teams at school. I'd just have to show him. One of these days, we'd play tennis, and I'd beat him.

We picked out tennis rackets and balls and tennis shoes. "We'll need bags, too," Dad said. "They'll be riding their bikes to the club during the week, while I'm at work."

"If we get Robin a bike," Josh said.

"Sure, we'll get her a bike. That'll be our next stop just as soon as we get through here." After he said that, I wanted to hurry and get the rest of the stuff and get out of there as soon as possible. He was really going to get me another bike today, just like he'd said he would.

We dropped off the tennis gear at home, and loaded the bike into the trunk. We got to the bike store, and Dad told the salesman the bike wasn't what I wanted.

The salesman looked at me and said, "Well, why don't you look around and see if there's something you do want?"

I walked around and looked at all the different

styles. I went over to a ten-speed just like Josh's. "I like this one," I said.

"You're too small to ride that," my father said. "I think you'd better look for something more your size."

"But I won't be small forever," I said. "I plan to grow next year."

"That's true, sir. If she hits a growth spurt, you'll be back in here next spring looking for another bike."

"I'll take that chance. I don't want her getting hurt because she's on a bike too big for her to control." He put his arm around my shoulders and guided me away from the bike I wanted. "Come on over here, honey. I'm sure you can find something you'll like just as much."

Well, he was wrong about that, too. I finally settled on a girl's three-speed. He said it would be easier for me to handle. I was sure I could have handled the ten-speed, but it didn't matter because he already had the salesman tying the three-speed on the top of the car.

I sat in the store and watched him through the window. Dad was giving him instructions and the salesman was tying the bike down. "It's a nice bike," Josh said coming up next to me.

"Yeah, but I could've ridden the ten-speed."

"I know."

"Yeah, but he doesn't."

"Tell you what. You can ride my bike some-times. Practice up on it and show Dad. Then he'll have to get you that ten-speed next year."

"You mean it?"

"Sure I do. You're my sister. We have to stick together." He slugged my shoulder. It was the first time since we'd gotten to my dad's house that it felt like I had my old brother back. I was glad, 'cause it was bad enough to lose Grandma and Grandpa. I didn't want to lose Josh, too.

5

Tennis was just as much fun as I had thought it would be. It was even better than badminton. Jeff was really nice, too. He kept saying I was a "natural." And I guess Josh liked the game okay, but he usually wanted to hurry up and get finished so he could go over to the pool and swim.

It was better living at Dad's house once we got busy with tennis. We'd ride our bikes to the clubhouse and play tennis a while or have a lesson, then Josh and I would swim for a couple of hours. Even though the pool was nice, tennis was my favorite. I was always looking for someone to play tennis with.

We'd finished the lesson one day and Josh was already in the pool. I was walking around the clubhouse looking for someone to play tennis with. Jeff came out of the pro shop.

"Thought you'd be in the pool by now," he said.

"I kind of hoped somebody might be looking for a partner."

"You know, Robbie, you're getting pretty darn good for — "

"Don't you dare say 'for a girl,' " I warned him. That's all I had heard from my dad since we'd moved here.

"I was going to say *for a beginner*." Jeff went back toward the pro shop. "Come here, I want to show you something." He pointed to a sign on the wall. "Did you see this?"

"What is it?"

"There's going to be a tennis tournament here next weekend. You want me to sign you up?"

"Oh, I'm not good enough to play in a tournament."

"Sure you are. I mean, I don't know that you could *win* your first tournament, but I coach other kids in your age group and I think you could hold your own against most of them. You could do real well in your division. If you want to find some tennis partners, this is a great way to advertise."

"Okay," I said. I practically flew out of the pro shop and over to the pool. Josh was doing a back dive off the board. I ran up to the edge of the pool and waited for him to pop up to the surface.

"Josh! Josh, guess what! There's a tennis tournament next weekend, and I'm going to play."

Josh folded his arms and rested his chin on the edge of the pool. "That's great, Rob. Hey, did you see that dive?"

39

"Yeah, it was pretty great, too." I told him.

"You coming in?"

"Naw, I think I'll go bat some balls against the wall or something. I need to work on my serve."

"Okay. See you later." He disappeared under the water. Grandpa always said Josh was part fish. I watched him gliding under the water and thought Grandpa might be right.

Hattie had made my favorite dinner: fried chicken. I was trying to find the wing when my father said, "Just take one, Robin. It isn't polite to finger them all."

"But I washed my hands."

"It doesn't matter. If you insist on a certain piece, use your fork. Not your fingers."

"Yes, sir."

"Hey, Dad," Josh said between mouthfuls, "did Robbie tell you she's going to play in a tennis tournament at the club next weekend?"

Dad looked at me, and I felt my face get red. "Is that right?" he asked. With my mouth full of mashed potatoes and gravy the best I could do was nod. "How about that? Are you playing, too, son?"

"Naw, I'm not that good."

"Well, surely if Robin can play you ought to be able to play, too."

"Swimming's more my thing, Dad."

"Tell you what, we'll play a match this weekend,

and I'll see if I can give you a few pointers. That way you and your sister can both enter the tournament."

"Gee, Dad, I don't know. I mean, tennis is okay. But I'm not crazy about it."

I swallowed my food and worked up my courage. "I'll play with you."

My father looked at me and smiled. "Well, if your brother feels up to it, we'll go to the club and bat the ball around. I'll stand both of you. How does that sound?"

"Sure," I said. But we never got a chance to play tennis before the tournament. My father had to work that weekend. I went to the club and batted the tennis ball against the wall and looked for someone who wanted to play, while Josh swam. I thought about my friend Stacy from back home. I wished she was here. She'd play with me. We'd always played badminton and Ping-Pong for hours. I knew she'd love tennis as much as I did.

Thinking about Stacy made me realize I wouldn't be seeing her when school started in a couple of weeks. She'd been my friend since first grade. While we didn't see much of each other during the summer, 'cause it was a long ways from Grandma and Grandpa's to her dad's farm, during the school year, I saw her every day, and we played together after school. I wouldn't be seeing *any* of my old friends at school. I'd be at a new school with new kids. I looked at all the strangers around me at the country club and realized I'd never felt so lonely before.

The Saturday of the tennis tournament it was hot and sunny. Hattie had bought me a thermos for good luck. She said she always saw the tennis players on TV drinking out of them, and she wanted me to have one, too. I was sorry she couldn't come, but it was her day off. That was the only time she got to see her grandchildren.

We got to the club early. Dad was playing golf. Josh was going to caddie for him. Dad looked at his watch. "The tournament starts at ten o'clock. We should be back in time to catch some of it."

Josh slugged me lightly on the arm. "Good luck."

"Take it easy," I said. "I'm going to need this arm during the tournament."

"Hey, I've seen you play. You could do better with one arm than I do with two."

I went over and started hitting a tennis ball against the wall. I had an hour and a half before the tournament started. A little bitty kid next to me was really slamming the ball hard. Of course, it bounced off the wall and he'd have to go chase it most of the time, but that didn't seem to matter to him.

I noticed another girl practicing against the wall. She looked like she was real good. She had long blonde hair, tied back so it wouldn't get in her way. It also made it easier to see her face. You could tell by the way she bit her bottom lip and never took her eyes off the ball that she had good concentration.

I went over to the court at ten o'clock. The sun had already started heating up the asphalt. There were separate divisions for ten-, twelve-, and sixteen-year-olds, and because the club isn't all that big, there were only a few kids in each division. Since I was eleven, I was playing in the division for twelve-year-olds, along with three other kids.

The girl I was playing looked as scared as I was feeling. But after I missed her first serve, I made myself pay attention and watch the ball, just like Jeff had taught me. After that first serve, it was all downhill for her. I won the match, and she never won a game. She couldn't control her swing. I kept her running all over the court. By the time we ended the match, she looked like she was about ready to drop over in the heat.

She ran off the court at the end of the match, and I heard her tell some woman that must have been her mom, "I hate this game! Why do you make me play? I told you I'm no good."

Jeff came over and clamped his hand on my shoulder. "Take a break. You've got a tough match coming up. If you win it you'll take first place in your division."

I went over to the snack bar and got a Popsicle. I looked around for my dad and Josh. I'd wished they could have been there to see my match. Maybe they would get back in time to see the next one. It was sure taking them a long time to play golf.

When I went back onto the court for my next match, I almost walked right off again. The girl across from me was the one with the blonde hair I'd seen earlier. I started to get real nervous. She looked about my age, but she was taller than me. (But that wasn't saying much. Most people my age are taller than me.)

Jeff was standing at the net. "Robin Welborn, this is Laney Walker. Laney, Robin Welborn. Good luck, you guys." He handed me two tennis balls and left the court.

Laney could slam a serve harder than anyone I'd ever played before. In the first set, she beat me as badly as I'd beaten the girl I'd played before. Now I knew how rotten that girl probably felt. All those people sitting around watching us get beat by somebody else.

I took some deep breaths and told myself to settle down before the next set. We played ten games in the second set. See, you have to keep playing until somebody wins six games. I'm not sure how I did it — maybe Laney was getting tired — but I won the second set 6–4.

The third set wasn't much of a set. I only won two games. Maybe I was the one getting tired now. After the fourth game, I looked over and saw my dad and Josh sitting on the grass watching me. Josh waved. I smiled and nodded my head in a kind of wave. When I looked back, the ball was already whizzing past me.

Maybe just knowing my father was sitting out there made me more nervous than usual, but I couldn't seem to do anything right after that. I had a couple good hits and a serve or two that wasn't bad, but mostly I just stood there and let her beat me. In fact, after my dad and Josh showed up, I didn't win another game that match. All I could think of was my dad, who probably figured he'd been right all along, that I wasn't very good at this game.

When it was over, Laney smiled and ran up to the net. I went up to shake her hand. She said, "Man, you're great. You want to play some time?"

She couldn't be talking to me. I hadn't been great. The last set, I'd been awful, as a matter of fact. "I don't know. I'm just starting. I'm not that good yet."

"But you will be," Laney said. We walked off

45

the court together. "Here, let me give you my phone number, and we'll get together and play."

I took the piece of paper she'd given me and held on to it real tight so I wouldn't lose it. It didn't even matter too much that I'd lost the match. After all, I still took second place. And more important, Laney wanted to play tennis with me! And she was really good. I ran off the court to tell Josh and Dad about it.

Dad put his arm around me. "Don't feel bad about losing, honey. It was a tough match."

"Yeah, I know. But guess what? Laney wants to play tennis with me. Isn't that great?"

"That isn't much of a challenge for her, is it?"

"Just think how good I'll be if we play every day. Next year, I might even be able to beat her."

"I'm just glad you found someone to play tennis with so you can stop bugging me," Josh said.

"Well, that wouldn't be much of a match anyway."

"What do you mean?" I asked. I thought maybe Jeff had told Dad that Josh didn't really like tennis very much.

"Well, after all, your brother is a boy. We can't expect you to be able to play tennis with him." He patted my shoulder. "Hey, let's get some lunch in the clubhouse. What do you say?"

I was too mad to say anything. I felt like if I jumped in the pool that very minute, the water would start boiling. Boy, did he have a lot to learn about girls and boys.

They went on into the clubhouse. I followed them inside. I didn't know how he would ever learn anything, though. He never gave me a chance.

6

Dad set his fork down and crossed his hands. He leaned across the table and said, "How would you kids like to go see your grandparents this coming weekend?"

I nearly choked on my mashed potatoes. "You mean it?"

"School starts in another week and Labor Day weekend is the last long weekend you'll have for a while. It might be nice to go for a visit. You know, let them know you're getting along all right down here."

It was hard to believe that school would be starting in just a week. I wondered what it would be like to go to school in a big city. It seemed a little scary. I would be starting middle school here, and back home sixth-graders were still in elementary school. One good thing about it, though: Laney and I were going to be in the same grade, at the same school. At least I'd know someone besides Josh.

"Well, how about it? Do I have any takers?" (That meant: Did we want to go?) I didn't know about Josh, but I sure wanted to.

"Yeah, sure," Josh said.

"Me, too!"

"Great. We'll call your grandparents tonight and let them know you're coming. You can fly into Lubbock on Friday and then fly home on Monday."

Lubbock is about an hour from Grandma and Grandpa's. I never thought about being able to fly there like that. I guess 'cause I always thought you had to fly to the place you were going to. We hadn't been on an airplane since we were really little. I didn't even remember what it felt like to fly. It would be exciting. And it would also give us more time to spend with Grandma and Grandpa. I had so much to tell them.

After dinner, I went upstairs and told Harold we were going home. He was real excited about seeing Grandma and Grandpa again. He wanted to start packing right away.

I was so excited the night before we left, I could hardly sleep. I kept thinking about how my bed back home was going to feel. First thing I wanted to do was pack some peanut butter sandwiches and go down to the creek for a picnic and swim in the pond. See, we have this old rope tied to a tree, and you can swing out over the water and drop in. It's lots of fun.

When we got off the plane I heard Josh saying, "There they are! I see Grandpa."

I stood on my tiptoes trying to see over the crowd. "Where?" All I could see were the people in front of me. I couldn't wait until I got tall some day.

The people started moving away from us and I saw Grandma and Grandpa, too. I ran toward Grandpa and he hugged me and swung me around in the air. He put me down, and I hugged my grandma. She felt just as soft and safe as she ever had. Boy, had I missed them.

I took hold of Grandpa's hand. He walked fast, and I liked to skip when I walked with him. He would let me swing hands with him. Grandma always said she didn't like me to do that with her because I just about pulled her over.

"I see you brought Harold," Grandpa said on the way to the car.

"Yep."

"Well, that's good. I don't 'spect he'd like it much if you went off and left him." Grandpa always understood about Harold better than any other grown person. Except maybe Hattie.

"So, how do you like Dallas?" Grandpa asked when we got in the car.

"It's okay," I said.

"It's neat," Josh said even louder. "I have my own ten-speed bike and we go to the country club every day. They have this great big swimming pool there with a high dive and everything. And when Dad and I go out to play golf, he lets me drive the cart sometimes. I'm getting really good, too. Want me to drive your car some time, Grandpa?"

Grandpa laughed. "Maybe later."

I listened to Josh talking about Dallas, and I was surprised. I guess I never knew he liked it that much. Then, I started thinking about how we hadn't been talking much since we'd moved there. Not like we used to when we lived at Grandma and Grandpa's.

But it was different when we lived here. There wasn't really anybody else around. We did almost everything together. Now, living with Dad, Josh and I were always off doing different things. I guess I told Hattie a lot of things I would have been telling Josh if he'd been around to talk to.

We got to Grandpa and Grandma's, and Josh opened the door almost before the car had stopped. "What do you have to eat, Grandma? I'm starved."

"We got lots of good things," Grandma said as she got out of the car and started to follow him in the house. "I baked an apple pie, but you have to wait till after lunch or you'll spoil your appetite."

"Not me, Grandma. I could eat that whole pie and still have room for lunch," Josh said.

"That's right, Grace. He's a growing boy," Grandpa said.

"Just the same, you leave that apple pie be till after lunch, you hear?" Grandma replied.

Grandpa put his arm around me. We sat down on the old porch swing. I loved rocking on that old porch swing with Grandpa. We always used to sit out there on warm nights and talk. Sometimes, we'd listen to the birds and insects, and Grandpa would tell me what kind they were. Other times, he would tell me about when he was a little boy. Those were my favorite times.

"I heard from your brother, but you haven't said much about how you like it in Dallas."

I shrugged my shoulders. "It's okay. I learned to play tennis."

"You did, huh?"

"And I'm pretty good."

"I'll just bet you are."

"I even played in a tournament and I got second place."

Grandpa nodded. "Not bad. Why, next year you'll be taking first place, huh?"

"Yeah. 'Course there weren't that many kids in

it. It was just a little tournament."

"Well, second place is second place."

"And there's Daddy's housekeeper, Hattie. I like her a lot." I swung my feet back and forth off the edge of the swing. I looked over at Grandpa. He was watching me. "She's not so . . . stuffy," I added.

Grandpa nodded. "I see. And is your daddy 'stuffy'?"

"Kind of, I guess. He's always telling me what I should do."

"Well, that's kind of his job. Daddies are supposed to tell you what you should do."

"I guess." I leaned against Grandpa and thought about how good it felt to be home again.

After lunch we went down to the swimming hole. I threw down my towel and grabbed hold of the rope. I swung way out over the water and let go. It's the greatest feeling to fly through the air like that. Then *splash!* You hit the water.

I came back up to the surface just as Josh hit the water. His head bobbed up, and I splashed him in the face. I swam as fast as I could for the shore. Josh caught up with me and got hold of my foot. He dragged me under, but I kicked loose and got out of the water before he could catch me.

By the time he got out on the bank, I was on the rope and back out into the water again. I sure had missed this old swimming hole.

Josh popped up next to me and rolled over to float on his back. I did the same thing. It was so cool to lay there on your back and look at the sky. The clouds drifted millions of feet above your head while the wind blew the leaves at the tops of the tall trees that surrounded the creek.

"I wish we could stay here forever," I said.

"Yeah. At least till dinnertime." Josh rolled over and started to tread water. "Come on." He splashed my face. "I'll race you to the bank."

We climbed out of the water. The hot Texas wind dried us off. I grabbed the rope. "Wanna go again?"

"I dunno. I wish we had a diving board like the one at the club. You can do a lot more stuff off a diving board than you can from that dumb old rope."

"I like the rope," I said grabbing hold and swinging out over the water. I didn't let go, though; I swung back onto the shore and stood up beside Josh again.

"Want to see who can jump the farthest?" I asked.

"No. This is boring. I wish we had our bikes here." Josh sat down in the grass. "Funny, we didn't used to get bored here."

"I'm not bored." I let go of the rope and sat down beside him. "There's lots of stuff to do here."

"Yeah, but not like Dad's house. You can ride bikes and go swimming in a real pool and drive the golf cart."

"Grandpa lets you drive the tractor," I said.

"Big deal. That's no fun."

"Oh, yeah, well, it's a lot more fun than a dumb old golf cart and a stinky old swimming pool that always smells like too much chlorine." I stomped off toward the house. Josh didn't come after me like I thought he would. He stayed out there a long time.

I was sitting on the porch drinking lemonade when he finally came back up to the house. He sat down on the swing beside me. "Sorry, Rob. I didn't mean to make you mad."

"It's okay."

"You don't like it much at Dad's house, do you?" I shook my head. "But why not?" he asked. "It's so awesome there."

"Maybe for you, but for me it's just a bunch of rules and silly ideas about what girls should do all the time."

"Yeah, I kind of noticed that. But you just have to show him you can do anything you want to. I mean, look at tennis. You're doing real good, and I can hardly serve the ball."

"That's because you don't like it. You could do it if you wanted to. And Dad knows that. What he doesn't know is that *I* can do it, too."

The screen door creaked. I looked up and saw Grandpa.

"I brought you some lemonade, Josh. Figured you could use some on a hot day like today." Grandpa sat down. He took off his old straw hat and wiped the back of his hand across his forehead. "It sure is a hot one. I could use a little dip in the old swimming hole myself today."

"The water feels real good," Josh said. "You want to walk down there?"

"I believe I just might." He stood up. Josh jumped off the porch. Grandpa stopped. "You coming, Robbie?" he asked.

"I think I'll see what Grandma's doing."

"I can tell you that. She's frying up a chicken," Grandpa said.

"My favorite!" I said, and Grandpa nodded. "I'll go see if she needs me to help."

I ran into the house. I could smell the chicken before I even got past the front door. There was nothing like the smell of Grandma's fried chicken.

The weekend went by faster than any weekend I ever remembered. It seemed like we'd just gotten there and it was already Monday and time to go home. I was feeling really bad about having to go back, but Josh acted like he couldn't wait to leave.

I was in my room packing my bag. Grandma knocked on the door. "Can I come in?"

"Sure."

She had something behind her back. "Got a surprise for you." She smiled, and her eyes were sparkling behind her glasses. She brought her hands out, and she was holding a new dress.

"I hope it fits. It's not easy when you don't have anyone to fit things to. And Grandpa's no help."

"It wouldn't fit Grandpa anyway," I said, and we both laughed. I unfolded the dress. It was light pink with little flowers all over it. It had a dropped waist with a gathered skirt. Grandma had crocheted a big collar around the neck.

"I hope you like it. I saw a dress like that in a magazine. You wouldn't believe how much they charge for a thing like that."

I held the dress up close and danced around the room. "I love it!" I ran to Grandma and hugged her.

"Well, I've always made you a new dress for the first day of school. I didn't want this one to be any different." Grandma wiped at the corner of her eye before she stuck her hankie back under the sleeve. "You'd better finish packing. We don't want you to miss that plane."

I watched her shut the door. Maybe she didn't want me to miss that plane, but I sure would have liked to. I folded the dress real carefully, and laid it in my suitcase. I watched it disappear as I zipped the bag shut, and I thought it was the prettiest dress I'd ever seen. I only wished Grandma would be there to see me wear it on the first day of school.

7

I pressed down the material of my dress with my hands and looked at myself in the mirror. It fit perfectly. Grandma had done a terrific job of guessing my size, considering I hadn't been around to try it on. I loved the dress. It looked so pretty. I opened my bedroom door and ran down to the kitchen to show Hattie.

"My, don't you look pretty," she said. "And your grandma made this for you?" She picked up the edge of the lace collar and looked at it. "She does real nice work, your grandma. Wish I had somebody could make nice things like that for me."

I smiled and went over to the table where Josh was already eating a huge bowl of cereal. He was reading the back of the cereal box. I'd noticed that he'd started doing that lately. Reading at the breakfast table, I mean.

"Good morning," my father said. "Everybody ready for the first day of school?"

Josh looked up from his box. "I am."

"How about you, Robin?" he asked as Hattie set a bowl on the table in front of me. I reached for the box of cereal.

"Hey, give that back. I wasn't done reading it," Josh said.

"I will. I have to get some first."

"If you want to read something in the morning, try the newspaper," my dad suggested. "It makes for much better reading than a cereal box, and you may actually come across something you can use in life."

I looked at Josh who looked at me and then down at his cereal, which was getting pretty soggy by now. I filled my bowl and set the box back over by Josh. He didn't pick it up again.

Dad looked at me. "What's that you're wearing?"

"It's my new dress."

He looked over at Hattie. "I don't remember that one in the things you showed me."

"It wasn't. Grandma made it," I told him.

"I thought I said Robin didn't need to wear homemade clothes, Mrs. Nelson. Isn't that why I sent you to the mall?"

"Yes, Mr. Welborn," Hattie said, tight-lipped.

"Robin, you go up and change into one of the new dresses Hattie bought you before you leave this morning."

I looked down at the dress Grandma had made

me that she was so proud of and I said, "No." Not loud or anything. Just real firm like my mind was made up.

"What did you say?"

"I said, 'No.' "

"Robin, honey, try to understand. This is a big city. Kids dress differently here. I just don't want you to feel out of place. You're not living on a farm anymore."

I stood up. "Well, I wish I was! I like it there. I like it lots better than here. And I'm wearing this dress today or I'm not going to school." I ran out of the kitchen and up to my room where I threw myself across the bed and sobbed.

I heard someone open the door. The bed moved when someone sat down on it, and I heard Josh say, "Dad says you can wear the dress."

I looked up at him. "Josh, let's go home. You said we could. You said if we didn't like it here we could go home."

"But I *do* like it here, Robbie. I think you will, too, if you give it a chance."

"I'm trying. I just miss home so much." I started to cry even harder.

"I know you do," Josh said. He put his arm around me and I cried all over his new shirt.

After Josh left, I stayed up in my room until it was almost time for school. I was gathering up my new school supplies when I heard a knock on the door. "Can I come in?" Hattie called.

"Sure."

She straightened the bedspread that Josh and I had messed up. Then she picked up Harold and held him close to her ear. "What's that, Harold? I couldn't quite hear you. Is that what you think?"

I ran to the foot of the bed. "What did he say?"

"He says you look very pretty in that new dress, and if he were a girl starting the sixth grade today, that's just the one he would have picked, too."

I ran over and hugged Hattie hard. She was soft to hug, just like Grandma. "I love you, Hattie."

"I love you, too, peanut. And don't you worry about a thing. You look real nice. Here, let me help you pull your hair back, and you'll be the prettiest girl in the sixth grade."

I was real glad I had worn the dress Grandma made me when I got to school. It was so scary, and just feeling the material made me feel closer to her and not so scared. The building was enormous. Hattie had brought us over for registration, and they had shown us around the school, but it looked different when it was full of kids. I looked around for Josh.

I was remembering our little school back home.

All the sixth-graders were in one class. And there were only three classrooms we had to worry about: the social studies area, math and science, and gym. This school was so big, and there was a different classroom for every period.

"Hey, Robin, what's your first period?" I thought there must be another Robin standing around me. I looked up to find Laney standing next to my locker.

I was never so happy to see somebody in my whole life. "Laney! Boy, am I glad to see you."

"So? What do you have first period?"

"Uh . . . English, room 202."

"With Mr. Leonard? Me, too." She grabbed my arm so hard I almost dropped my books. "Come on."

For the rest of the day I just followed Laney like a baby duck follows its mother. She introduced me to all kinds of kids. I couldn't remember half of their names. There were more kids in my English-social studies block than we had in the whole sixth grade back home. And I knew all the kids back home because we'd been going to school together since we'd started. This middle school was even bigger than our old high school.

I was walking to lunch with Laney and two other girls named Alex and Ginger. They were busy talking about who had gotten cuter this year and which teachers were going to be really tough. We went into the noisy lunchroom. "You buying?" Laney asked.

"Buying?" I wasn't sure what she meant. Hattie only gave me enough money for one lunch. I thought it sounded like she wanted me to pay for all of them. I didn't know what to say.

"You know," Ginger said. "Are you going to buy your lunch or did you bring one from home?"

"Oh," I said with relief. "I'm buying."

"Then let's get in line," Laney said. We started toward the line and Laney said, "Oh, wait, I forgot my money." She ran back over to the table where we'd set our stuff down. Alex and Ginger went on to get in line. "Go on, I'll be right there," Laney told me.

I hurried to catch up with Alex and Ginger. I heard Alex say, "Geez, where did Laney meet her?"

"You know Laney. She's always picking up strays. I guess she just moved here."

"From where? Mars? And did you get a load of that dress?" I touched the material of my skirt and felt my face get hot. "What a geek!" They both laughed.

Laney ran up beside us. "Sorry. Hey, what do you guys have after lunch?" Their voices blended together into a blur. I didn't listen. I didn't care. I hoped I didn't have them in any of my classes for the rest of the day. Girls like that made me sick. They were so nice to you to your face, and then they were mean when they thought you weren't around. If that's what Laney and her friends were like, I didn't want any part of them.

I thought about Stacey again. I was wishing I had seen her when we went to visit my grandparents. She was the one I always ate lunch with at my old school. I missed her more than ever now.

After the four of us had eaten we put our trays on the conveyor belt and went back to the table to get our books. "You were awful quiet during lunch," Laney said. "Is everything okay?" I nodded. "Well, then, I'll see you sixth period." We picked up our books just as the bell rang.

I got lost trying to find the drama room. Drama was my sixth period class. I was really excited about it. We didn't have any drama classes until high school back home. I thought it would be the one thing that I would like about Dallas.

"Robin, over here!" I saw Laney sitting with Alex. They both waved to me. I pretended I didn't see them. I sat down next to the door just before the bell rang. The teacher, Mrs. Johnson, looked like she was going to be really nice. We did theater games all period, and then she assigned us a pantomime for the next day.

Laney caught up with me after class. "Hey, how come you avoided me all period?"

"I didn't," I lied.

"You've been acting funny since lunch. Did I do something?" I shook my head. "Well, then what's wrong?" Laney asked. "You aren't one of those moody people, are you?"

"No. I'm just a geek," I said, looking straight at Alex. I walked away from them and went to my locker. Josh came up just as I was stuffing my last folder in.

"So? How was the first big day at Wyman Middle School?"

"Terrible. How was yours?"

He slung his backpack over his shoulder. "Not bad." We walked out of the school together. I saw Ginger at the front door.

"Have you seen Alex or Laney?" she asked.

"Last I saw they were outside the drama room," I said.

"Who's that?" Josh asked after she ran back inside the building.

"Some friend of Laney's."

"She's kind of cute." I looked back, but all I saw was the sun reflecting off the glass doors. Ginger was long gone.

Kind of cute? I guess she was. Her long brown hair was curly and full, and she had real big brown eyes. I guess if I didn't know her, I'd think she

66

was kind of cute, too. But since I did know her, all I could think was that she was kind of mean.

Josh and I went on the bike trail after school. We met Josh's friends Nick and Kyle there, and the four of us rode along the creek and looked for water snakes and frogs. I liked Nick and Kyle a lot better than any of the sixth-grade girls I'd met so far.

The phone was ringing when we came in the kitchen door. "I'll get it," I yelled. I was surprised to hear Laney's voice on the other end.

"Look, Robin, I don't know what Alex and Ginger said to you, but don't be mad at me."

"I'm not."

"Well, you sure have a funny way of showing it. After you left I asked Alex what you were talking about, and she said she didn't have any idea. But I think she does."

"It doesn't matter."

"It matters to me. I like you, Robin. I want us to be friends. Please don't be mad at me because of something Alex and Ginger said, okay?"

"Okay."

"Hey, what are you going to do for your pantomime tomorrow?" she asked.

"I don't know. I haven't thought about it yet. What are you going to do?"

Laney started telling me about her idea for her pantomime, and then we talked about our English teacher who looked quite a bit like George Washington, and before I knew it my dad was coming home for dinner. I had forgotten all about Alex and Ginger, and I wasn't mad at Laney anymore.

We sat down to dinner, and the first thing my dad wanted to know was how we liked school. He hadn't said any more about this morning. He acted like it had never even happened.

"I have this really neat art class," Josh told him. "The teacher's real funny. She's cute, too, Dad. You ought to see her."

"I can hardly wait for open house." He smiled at Josh. He looked at me. "How did you like school, Robin?"

"It's okay. I got lost a lot at first. Then Laney helped me out, and I was okay."

"Who's Laney?"

"You know, the girl from the country club Robin played tennis with at the tournament," Josh explained.

"Oh, yes, I remember her. Well, I'm glad to see you're making friends."

"Hey, Dad, I think I'm going to go out for football. They have a team meeting tomorrow after school."

"That's great. I loved playing football when I was in school. I don't know if your mother told you or not, but I went to A&M on a football scholarship."

"No kidding?" Josh said. You could see he saw my dad through new eyes once he got that bit of information. My dad sat back with this goofy grin on his face like he'd just found out about the scholarship himself. "I didn't know you played football," Josh said.

"There's a lot you don't know about your old man."

"What position did you play?"

"Center."

"Man, that's neat. Wait'll I tell Nick."

"Tell you what. After dinner, we'll go upstairs and I'll show you some of my old yearbooks."

"Neat." Josh shoveled in the rest of his dinner just so he could get upstairs and dig through a bunch of smelly old yearbooks to look at pictures of my dad in a football uniform. I didn't think it was all that neat. I mean, it wasn't like he ever played for the Dallas Cowboys or anything. Now *that* would have been neat. I would have even gone upstairs to see that.

8

No matter how busy he was, my dad managed to get to all of Josh's football games. Sometimes Josh didn't even hardly play, but we went to the game anyway.

We sat in the stands with the twenty-five or so other parents who showed up for the games. I usually looked around to see if there was anybody I knew, while Dad watched the game. When something real good or real bad happened he would tell me why it was good or why it was bad. I was learning a little about football, anyway. But I was also learning something about myself. I didn't like football very much.

One Friday afternoon, Josh's team actually won a game. When the clock finally ran out, Dad grabbed me and hugged me. I hugged him back, and pretty soon I was laughing and jumping up and down like everybody else.

"This calls for a celebration," he said. "I'm taking you and your brother out to dinner tonight. Any place you want to go. You name it."

"Okay," I said. He put his arm around my shoulders and we walked down to the field to tell Josh we'd be waiting for him in the car.

Josh was even more excited than we were. The whole team was running around yelling and slapping each other on the shoulder pads. Even though it was only a junior high game, everyone was as excited as if they'd won a state championship. Even me.

Josh came running over to us. "Did you see it?" he yelled. "Wasn't it great?"

"Terrific!" my dad answered. "Now that you guys figured out how to win, do it again." He reached over and hugged Josh around the neck. "Tell you what, champ; we're going out to celebrate. What do you say?"

"Gee, Dad, a bunch of us from the team were going to go out for pizza." Josh looked back at the team that was still going wild on the field. Then he looked at me and Dad. "But I'll tell them I've got other plans. I can go out with them next time."

Dad clasped Josh on the shoulder. "There may be other games, but there won't be other first wins. You go on with the team."

"Really?"

"Really. Now get going before they take off and leave you."

Dad looked at me after Josh ran off to the locker

room. "Well, kid, looks like it's just the two of us. What do you say to a date with your old man?"

"Sure," I said.

He put his arm out for me to take it. "Shall we, madam?" I put my hand on his arm and he walked me off the field.

We walked all the way to the car like that. He opened my door for me and then went to his side to get in. He put the keys in the ignition and stopped to look at me. "Where do you want to go?"

"I don't care."

"Come on, you can be more imaginative than that. What do you feel like eating? Steak? Mexican? Italian? Hamburgers? You name it."

"Steak," I said.

"Then steak it is!" He backed the car out of the parking lot. I sneaked peeks at him while he was driving. He was whistling along with the radio. Maybe he was just happy because they'd won the game, but he didn't seem like the same person who was always reminding me what not to do around the house.

We went to a place called Steak and Ale. We had to sit in the bar for a few minutes because there weren't any tables. Dad ordered a drink for himself and a Shirley Temple for me. "You ever had a Shirley Temple before?" he asked. I shook my head no. "You'll like it." He patted my hand.

"Trust me." Looking at him in the soft light of the restaurant, I believed I could.

That was the greatest dinner I ever had. Not because the food was so great. I mean, it was pretty good, but I just felt really special. My dad actually spent a whole evening talking only to me. He wanted to know how I liked my classes and how school was going. He asked about things back home at Grandma's house. And he really listened to everything I said.

Then he told me about when he was a kid. He told me about how they'd won the district football championship and then got beaten in the state play-offs. I could understand why Josh spent so much time looking at his old yearbooks up in the attic. It wasn't the yearbooks that counted. It was just spending time with Dad like this.

I hated to see the waitress bring the check. I was sorry our "date" was over. On the way home, Dad was listening to the oldies station he likes and singing along with the radio. Every once in a while, he would say, "Oh, this was popular when I was a junior. I remember . . ." and he'd tell me all about it.

When we pulled the car into the garage that night, my dad looked different to me. He was a real person with memories and feelings, just like Grandpa.

He opened the back door for me. As I started into the house he grabbed my hand and bowed. "Thank you for a wonderful evening, madam. We must do it again some time." Then he kissed my hand. I just looked at him and smiled.

Saturday was one of those fall days you can't wait for when it's scorching outside in the middle of August. I set down the book I'd been reading and looked out my window. Why was I wasting such a great day sitting in my room?

I went downstairs to see if Josh wanted to go on a bike ride. He was in the family room with Dad watching some ball game on TV. I went over and sat on the couch beside him. He acted like he didn't even see me come into the room.

I looked over at him. He and my dad were sitting forward, leaning into the TV. They looked like they were about to hear Ed McMahon announce the winner of the ten-million-dollar sweepstakes, and they thought it might be them. (Grandma listened to that every year. Grandpa told her it was foolish, and she wasn't going to win, and she told him she just might. And if she did, she wasn't going to share any of it with him.)

Josh and Dad let out a yell, and Josh jumped up so fast he nearly knocked the coffee table over. I almost had a heart attack. Josh turned to me. "Man, did you see that? What a play!"

"Guess I missed it," I mumbled.

"Here. Watch the instant replay." I looked at the TV. Some guy caught the football and started running. Another guy knocked him down. Big deal. That's what's supposed to happen in a football game, isn't it?

A commercial came on and Josh sat back down. "Hey," I said, "you wanna go for a bike ride?"

"You kidding?" Josh looked over at Dad and rolled his eyes like I was some kind of nut. "Do you know who's playing?"

"I give up."

"Texas and Texas Tech," he said, like he'd just told me something really important.

"Oh." I looked at my dad. "Do you want to go on a bike ride? It's really nice out."

He smiled at me. "Not now, honey. They're going into the last quarter. Maybe later." Then the commercial was over, and they were back into the game again. I studied my dad's face for a minute, trying to find the man who'd taken me to dinner last night. But he was gone now, and the other dad was back. I got up off the couch.

"Hey, where you going? The score's tied," Josh said.

"I'm not sure I can handle the suspense." I went out into the kitchen and cut myself a piece of Hattie's chocolate cake. Hattie didn't work on the weekends, and I sure got lonely for her. We usually went out to dinner on Saturday nights. On Sundays we'd either eat out or my dad would grill something on the barbecue. I liked Hattie's cooking much better.

I got my bike out of the garage and peddled off down the bike trail. It was a perfect day for a bike ride. The red and yellow leaves that had fallen on the trail crunched under my bike tires.

I got off my bike at the bridge and sat down to watch the creek run by below me. There were big rocks in the creek, and the water had to split apart and rush around them. I was sitting there staring at that water, and I got this crazy idea that Josh and I were kind of like that water. Just running along minding our own business. My dad was like the rock. He just popped up out of nowhere and split us up. I watched the water bubble and roll underneath me. I got up and walked to the other side of the bridge where the water settled back down. That is, until the next big rock got in its way. Would Josh and I ever run smooth again?

I got on my bike and rode over to the country club. I went to the tennis courts. I'm not sure why. I didn't even have my racket. I saw Laney playing tennis with some man. I sat down and watched them play. The man kept yelling things to her like "Good volley" or "Nice shot." When she missed an easy backhand shot, he ran up to the net and showed her how to grip the racket and move into a backhand shot. I wonder if he was a new tennis coach at the club.

They finished the match, and I got up to go. Laney saw me. "Robin! When did you get here?"

"A little while ago."

"Did you bring your racket? You want to play?"

"I didn't bring it," I said, wishing like anything I had.

"You can use mine," the man said. He had one of those real expensive rackets that you buy at the sporting goods stores. The kind they string just for you. You know, like the pros use.

"I better not," I said looking at the racket in his hand.

"Please. You'd be doing me a favor. Laney's about got me worn out." He held the racket toward me.

"Okay," I said taking the racket. "I'll be really careful."

"I know you will. Just give it to Laney when you finish." He turned and kissed Laney on the top of her head. "I'll wait for you in the clubhouse, honey."

Obviously this guy was not a tennis instructor. I must have had a crazy look on my face. Laney started laughing. "Oh, I almost forgot. Robin, this is my dad. Daddy, this is my friend Robin. I told you about her."

Her dad looked at me. "I recognized you from the tournament last month. You think I'd give my racket to just anyone?" He winked at Laney. "See you later, princess."

I watched him go into the clubhouse. That was Laney's dad? What was he doing out here on a Saturday afternoon when Texas was playing Texas Tech? He had actually been playing tennis with her. I thought about how my dad still hadn't found time to play tennis with me.

"Your dad's real nice," I said.

"Yeah, he is, isn't he?"

"Do you guys play very much?"

"Just about every weekend. My mom doesn't really like tennis much, and Daddy loves it. That's how I learned to play."

"But what about tennis lessons?"

"Oh, yeah," Laney shrugged, "I had those. But I really learned to play with my dad on the weekends. He used to play in college."

"Oh. My dad played football," I said. I guess dads just liked to teach their kids what they liked best. And, I had to face it, my dad didn't think much of tennis.

Laney beat me, as usual, but I was getting better. I had managed to win one set. I liked playing with her because she was good, and I knew if I could beat her, no one could touch me, not even my dad, if he ever decided to play.

"You want to go in the clubhouse and get something to drink?" Laney asked.

"Sure."

We went inside and I gave the racket back to Mr. Walker. "Who won?" he asked.

"Not me," I said.

"She did great, though. She beat me one set. That's pretty good. Robin just started playing this summer."

"No kidding?"

"Yeah, I just moved down here with my dad."

"Does he play tennis? We could play doubles some Saturday."

"Maybe after football season is over," I said.

Laney's dad smiled. "Well, you're welcome to come out and bat the ball around with us any time you want."

"Thanks," I said. But I would have felt funny. I think Mr. Walker was just being nice. I really hoped that my dad might play tennis with me after football season was over, but I wasn't sure. I was wishing I had thought about asking him last night when things were different. But this morning, everything was back like it was before.

Laney and I sat down at a table over by the windows. The golf course stretched out below us clear into the distance. "Do you have any brothers or sisters?" I asked.

"A little brother, Jason. He's eight and he's a brat." Laney rolled her eyes toward the ceiling. "I wish he were older, like your brother. Josh is so cute. And he seems really nice, too."

If she'd said that about Josh two months ago, I would have said he was the greatest brother in the world. But lately, he was a lot more interested in being a son than in being a brother. He never wanted to do anything anymore unless it was with my dad.

"He's okay," I said.

"You're lucky. Jason can drive you up the wall in about ten minutes. He's always coming in my room and messing with my stuff. Sometimes, I'd like to strangle him."

"Does he play tennis, too?" I asked.

"Are you kidding? He's more the type for football and other deadly games."

"What does your dad think about that?"

"Oh, he thinks it's okay. He goes to Jason's games and takes the team out for pizza when they win just like all the other dads."

"They have teams for eight-year-olds?" They didn't even have teams for the junior high back home.

"Sure. Pop Warner Football. It's throughout the city, I think. It's like the baseball teams in the summer."

Laney started telling me how they had cheerleaders for the teams and how she had been a cheerleader when she was younger. My mind drifted away, and I started thinking about how Laney's dad managed to go to football games and still play tennis with her. Then I thought about my dad. The first real thing we'd done together since I'd moved here was the night before. I was almost wishing he'd never paid any attention to me at all. I kind of wished he had just taken Josh off to live with him and left me at my grandparents. That way, I wouldn't care if he paid attention to me or not.

Laney took hold of my arm and shook it. "Robin, are you listening to me?"

"What?"

"I said, are you going to try out for the play next week?"

"I don't know. I'm kind of nervous."

"Who isn't?" Laney said. "You really should. You're one of the best in our theater class. You'd be perfect for the part of the princess."

We were going to do a children's play called *The Princess and the Goblins*. We would put it on for the grade schools. We were also planning to do a performance for the parents one night.

"Are you going to try out?" I asked.

"Sure."

"For what part?" I didn't want to try out for the same part as Laney. She was really good.

Losing to her in tennis was bad enough; I didn't want to compete against her in everything we did.

"I want to be the Goblin Queen. I love that part."

I couldn't imagine sweet Laney playing the evil Goblin Queen. Laney was so pretty. I started thinking about it. It *would* be fun. Maybe Grandma and Grandpa would come see it. My dad might even stop watching Josh play football long enough to come see me. He'd find out girls *could* do something.

By the time we left the clubhouse my mind was made up. I was trying out for the play. The easy part was deciding to try out. The hard part was going to be doing it. I wasn't as sure as Laney that I was all that talented. But Laney had invited me over to her house the next afternoon to read through the script. Her mom had done some plays in high school and she was going to help us. I told Laney I'd be there.

"Do you want to ask your dad first and call me later this afternoon?" Laney wondered.

I was sure it would be okay. After all, tomorrow was Sunday and the Dallas Cowboys would be on TV. I was sure they wouldn't miss me. I probably could have gone to the moon for all they cared, as long as my trip didn't mess up the reception on the TV set.

9

It was so hot in the theater room. The air hung over our heads and seemed almost too heavy to breathe. There were so many kids there. I hadn't thought about kids from other classes coming to the audition. Laney's mom said she would give me a ride home when we finished. I had told Hattie I might be late for dinner. But from the looks of it, I'd be lucky to get home by midnight.

I watched a lot of other girls read for the part I wanted. They all seemed so good. I decided trying out was a bad idea. I would just watch Laney audition and go home. Mrs. Johnson looked around the room. "Is there anyone else who wants to read for the Princess before we go on?"

Laney elbowed me in the ribs. I looked over at her and she nodded her head fiercely toward Mrs. Johnson. "Okay then," she said.

"I would," I said before I could chicken out again.

"All right, Robin. Come on up." I took the

script. It shook in my hands. I told myself, *calm down*, but I didn't listen. The whole time I was reading, the script was shaking, and I just knew that everyone in the room saw it, too. If Laney's mom hadn't been giving me a ride home, I would have run out of that room and all the way home by myself.

Laney did really well. I was sure she would get the Goblin Queen. She sounded so mean. But it was a funny-mean. It wouldn't be a scary play for little kids to watch.

It was almost six o'clock when everyone finished auditioning. Mrs. Johnson picked up the extra copies of the scripts lying around the room. "I'll have the cast posted in the morning. You can stop by on your way to first period." No one moved. "Thank you all for coming," she said. She turned around and went to her desk. We all finally took the hint and started leaving.

We had hardly gotten out the door before Laney was grabbing onto my arm and jumping up and down. "You were terrific!"

"No, I wasn't."

"Yes, you were. I bet you get the part. I was watching Mrs. Johnson's face when you read, and she was smiling. I think she really liked you."

"I know she *had* to like you," I told her. "You were the best one for the Goblin Queen."

"You really think so? Oh, I hope you're right.

I want that part so bad. Hey, what if we both get parts? We'll be in the play together! It'll be so much fun."

"Even if I don't get a part, I'll work backstage or something. I just want to be in it."

"You'll get a part." Laney laughed and looped her arm around my neck. "You are such a dope. You're a great actress, and you don't even know it."

I came into the kitchen, and Hattie was dishing up dinner. "How did it go?"

"How did what go?" my dad asked. He looked like he had just gotten home from work. He had loosened his tie and was rolling up his sleeves. He always did that before he sat down to dinner.

"Robbie had a big audition today."

"It wasn't that big," I said.

"It looked pretty big to me," Josh said as he came into the kitchen. His hair was still wet from the shower. "There were about a hundred kids in there."

"Not that many, really," I said. I was wishing I had never told anyone about it. If I had just told them I was going to watch Laney they would never have to know I'd tried out. Now they were all expecting me to get a part.

"There were lots of kids better than me," I said so no one would be surprised when I ended up pulling the curtain instead of being on the stage.

"I don't believe that," Josh said. "Robbie's a real good actress. She had the lead in the Thanksgiving Day Pageant every year."

"Well, that's really something, Robin. I didn't know you were a budding actress."

"How was practice?" I asked, knowing that if I just brought up football I could get them off any topic in the world. Sure enough, it worked. The rest of the meal was spent talking about football and how they were going to do in Friday's game and then eventually how they were going to do next year.

I wondered what next year would be like for me. It seemed a hundred years away. I missed home. I didn't know if I would be able to spend the next six years here.

I wondered what it would be like after Josh graduated and went off to college. Then it would just be me and my dad. I thought about dinner last week and our "date." Could it be like that all the time after Josh went away to college? Or would we be so far apart by then we'd never have anything to talk about?

I didn't even get to the theater room the next morning before I knew. Laney came running up the hall toward me. She was yelling something about "made it!" She wrapped her arms around me and started spinning around in big circles in the hall.

"That's great," I said. "I knew you would."

Laney stopped turning me around. We both stood there trying to get our balance. "Didn't you hear me? I said *we* made it!"

I couldn't believe my ears. I raced down the hall to see for myself. Sure enough. Right there on the paper it said PRINCESS: ROBIN WELBORN. Big as life.

I raced back down the hall, and this time *I* grabbed Laney. "We made it!"

Ginger and Alex came up to us. "Man, you guys are making enough noise. What's going on?"

"We're in the play," Laney said.

"No kidding?" Alex answered. "I was going to try out for that, but I didn't."

"What play?" Ginger wanted to know.

"Some children's thing," Alex explained. "I just didn't have time. Anway, I think it's great you two got parts."

"Yeah, we'll come see it," Ginger said. But you could tell by the way she said it that they wouldn't be there. I didn't want them there anyway.

Laney watched them walk down the hall. "I can't believe we were all best friends last year."

"It's because of me. I don't think they like me very much."

"Well, that's okay. Because I like you a lot."

The first period bell rang and we ran off to class. I could hardly concentrate that whole day. I couldn't wait to get home and tell Hattie about the play.

"Hattie. Hattie!" I yelled coming in the back door. I was surprised to see my dad sitting at the kitchen table.

"What did I tell you about calling Mrs. Nelson by her first name?" he asked.

"I'm sorry. I didn't know you were home."

"Robin, when I ask you to do something, I have a good reason. Now, whether I am home or not, rules are rules. They don't change just because I'm not home."

"Yes, sir. Where is . . . Mrs. Nelson?"

"Shopping. She'll be back any minute now."

"You're not sick, are you?" I asked.

"No, of course not."

"That's good."

"I just decided I've been working much too hard lately. I wanted to spend some time with my children."

"Really?"

Dad scooted his chair back from the table. "Sit down." He pointed to another chair. I sat down.

I looked at the wood grain of the table. I traced the wavy line with my finger across the smooth surface.

"So, how was school today?" he asked.

"Good."

"How are your classes? How was that test in history that you told me about last week?"

"I got an eighty-two."

"Not bad," he said, nodding his head.

"No, it's good. Most of the kids got in the sixties."

"Good for you then. I'm glad to see that you're not having any trouble keeping up."

"What do you mean?"

"It's just that sometimes when you've gone to those little country schools the education is lacking, and when you try to make the jump to a bigger school, you have trouble keeping up. That's one of the reasons I'm glad you were able to move to Dallas with me. It'll give you a real head start on those other kids from small towns when you get ready to go off to college someplace."

"I'm not having any trouble," I told him. "We had good teachers back home."

"I'm sure you did." He put his hand over the top of mine. "Robin. You keep referring to your grandparents' house as 'back home.' But *this* is your home now. I wish you'd start thinking about it like that. I don't think you're going to be happy here unless you can start to feel like you *are* home. I want you to be happy. I really do."

"Okay," I said. But I knew saying it was one

thing. Actually feeling it was something else.

The back door slammed, and Hattie came in. She set the groceries down on the counter. "Well?" she asked.

"Well, what?" my father said.

Hattie looked back at me. "Did you get it?" I couldn't keep the smile off my face. I bobbed my head up and down like a crazy person. "You did?" Hattie ran over to the chair, and I jumped up. She folded her big soft arms around me and picked me right up in the air. "We got us an actress, Mr. W."

"Oh, that's right. The part. You got it, huh?" Hattie set me back on the floor.

"Uh-huh," I said.

"Well, that's wonderful. We'll have to go see it. What's the name of it again?"

"*The Princess and the Goblins*. I play the princess."

"Well, isn't that nice," he said.

"I'll say it is," Hattie agreed. "I believe this calls for something special. And I know just the thing. I know a certain little girl who happens to love my brownie supreme. That sounds like just the ticket for a princess." Hattie squeezed my shoulder.

"Sounds to me like you'd better get on the phone and call your grandparents. I'm sure they'll want to make plans to come up, too." Dad looked at his watch. "Your grandfather is probably still out in the fields. Maybe you should wait until after dinner. What do you think?"

"I think it's a great idea! I'll call them just as soon as we finish eating." I surprised us both by throwing my arms around my daddy's neck and giving him a great big hug. I felt his strong arms close around me.

I ate so fast I hardly tasted my dinner. I wanted to call my grandparents with the news and hear what they had to say. I missed them so much.

Hattie hadn't even cleared away the last dish before I was on my feet. "Can we call them now?"

"Who?" Josh asked.

"Grandma and Grandpa. We're going to call them tonight so I can tell them about the play."

"Let me say 'hi,' too. Then I got to meet a bunch of the guys in the park in a few minutes," Josh said.

We went into the family room, and Dad dialed the phone. It started ringing, and he handed it to me.

" 'Lo," the voice on the other end said.

"Grandpa?" I said.

"Robbie, is that you?"

I giggled. "Yep."

"Mother," he hollered, "get on the other extension. The children are on the phone."

"How've you been?" Grandpa asked.

"Okay."

"Robbie, is that you?" Grandma said, picking up the phone.

"Of course, it's her. We already established that. What I'm trying to find out now is how she's been."

"I've been great," I said. "Guess what?"

"What?" both of them said in unison.

"I got a part in the play the theater class is doing next month. Can you come see it?"

"Well, I don't know. When would it be?" Grandpa asked. "We might have something going on."

My heart sank. Then I heard Grandma say, "Oh, stop teasing that child! Of course we'll come."

"You bet! What could be more important than seeing our little Robbie make her big debut on the Dallas stage?" I giggled again.

"And Grandma, you don't have to be scared when you get here," I told her. "I've been here two months, and I haven't seen a single weirdo or murderer."

"Oh, you." Grandma laughed. Daddy looked at me like I was crazy. Then he looked over at Josh.

"I'll tell you later," Josh said. He reached out his hand to me. "Let me talk now."

I hated to give up the phone. I wanted to climb right into the wires and shoot across to their house, just like my voice did. I thought how neat it would be if I could really do that.

"I have to go now," I said. "Josh wants to talk. But I want to talk to you again before you hang up."

"All right," Grandpa said.

I gave the phone to Josh. "I've never seen you so excited," my dad said. "I like seeing you this happy. I like that smile of yours. I hope it becomes a permanent thing around here."

"Me, too," I said.

I waited impatiently while Josh told them all about football and told them they'd have to see a game when they came. He even said maybe they would get tickets to see the Cowboys and go to a real football game. Finally he said good-bye and handed the phone back to me.

"You take care of yourself now," Grandpa said.

"I will," I promised. "And you take care of yourself, too."

"It was good hearing from you," Grandpa said.

"Did you wear your new dress yet?" Grandma wanted to know.

"Uh-huh. The first day. Everyone talked about it," I said, thinking about what Alex and Ginger said. Then I felt a little guilty about lying to her. But it wasn't really a lie. They *had* talked about the dress. I just hadn't told her what they'd said.

"Well, we can't wait to see you children,"

Grandma said. "It gets awfully lonely in this old house without you here."

"It gets awful lonely in this old house, too," I said. I knew I was going to start crying any minute, and I didn't want to start bawling all over the telephone and ruin the whole night.

"I love you," I said.

"We love you, too," Grandma said. "You sleep tight."

"And don't let the bedbugs bite," Grandpa said.

I had to hang up real fast and go to my room. That's what they always used to say when we went to bed at night. I lay down on my pillow and cried. Not very loud or anything. Tears just slid out of my eyes. I hugged Harold real tight until I felt better.

I rolled over onto my back and set Harold on my stomach. "I just talked to Grandma and Grandpa," I told him. "They're coming for a visit."

Harold was real glad to hear that. He missed Grandma and Grandpa a whole bunch. I hugged him so hard I could feel his button eyes biting into my cheek. "Don't you be sad, Harold. Grandma and Grandpa are coming, and everything's gonna be okay."

10

With play practice, Josh wasn't the only one getting home just in time for dinner anymore. I liked rehearsing a lot. It was even more fun than I thought it would be. The only bad part about it was not getting to see nearly as much of Hattie. I missed our afternoon talks. I used to come home from school and sit on the counter in the kitchen and talk to Hattie while she made dinner. She would ask all about my day and really want to know how it went.

I was beginning to figure out, with my dad, when he asked how my day went, what he really wanted to hear was "fine" or "okay" or "great!" He never asked me why my days were okay or terrific or terrible. I think the only reason he asked me about them at all was so he'd have something to say to me. The more time I spent around him, the more I felt like he wasn't exactly sure what to do with me.

I remembered one particular night. I'd been in

my room learning my lines, and I came down to the kitchen to get a glass of milk. I heard my dad and Josh talking. I stopped outside the door and listened to them. Josh was telling my dad about something that had happened in his gym class, and my dad was actually laughing about it. He sounded like he had the night we went to dinner together. I listened a while. I kind of wanted to go inside, but I felt like an intruder so I stayed out.

Finally I went back up to my room without my glass of milk. I was wishing things could have been different. I wanted the three of us to get along, but my father didn't seem to treat me the same when Josh was around.

It was hard to believe the play was only a week away. It was the fastest that time had gone since I moved to Dallas. I sat in the audience while they rehearsed the second scene. I'd made a lot of new friends since the play started. I wondered if we would all still be friends when it was over?

Mrs. Johnson called a break before we started the third scene. Laney came and sat down next to me. "Hey, don't look so sad. You're about to become a star. When are your grandparents coming?"

"They'll be here Friday. I can hardly wait. I want you to meet them. You'll really like them.

My grandpa is such a tease. And my grandma is the best cook in the whole world."

"What about Hattie?"

I thought about that a minute. "Well, she's second. One of these nights I'll have you over to dinner, and you can see for yourself. Hey, I have an idea! Why don't you come over to dinner while my grandparents are here?"

"That would be neat. I really want to meet them."

"Okay." I was so excited. Laney was going to get to meet my grandparents, and they would get to meet her. Laney was the first person I'd asked to dinner since I'd come to Dallas. It wasn't like Laney had never been to my house. She'd come home with me a couple of times, but my dad had never been there. So she hadn't met him, either.

I didn't get a chance to ask my dad about Laney coming to dinner. It turned out he had a bigger surprise of his own. During dinner it was very quiet at the table. It seemed like we all had something on our minds, and no one wanted to be the first one to talk.

Hattie brought out dessert, and my dad picked up his fork. He slid it into the soft white cake. He put the cake in his mouth. Then he set the fork down next to his plate. I wondered if he was going to eat his cake, because if he didn't want it I would eat it for him. I loved Hattie's white cake.

"Uh . . ." Josh and I both looked at him. "Something has come up, and I'm going to be leaving the country for a week or so. We're having some trouble in South America. Since I was there so many years, they figured who better to straighten things out?"

"When will you go?" Josh asked.

"Wednesday morning. Hattie's going to stay here while I'm gone."

"But what about the play?" I asked. "It's Friday night."

"I'm sorry, Robin, I'd love to be there for it, but this is something that just can't wait. You'll have to tell me all about it when I get home. How will that be?"

I had to nod my head because I didn't trust my voice. I knew I was going to cry if I said another word. Until that minute, I didn't know how much I wanted him to be there.

"I'll also miss seeing your grandparents. I thought I'd give them a call tonight and explain things so they won't be surprised when they show up and I'm not here."

"Can I talk to them, too?" I asked.

"Sure. We'll call them after we finish eating." He picked up his fork again and finished his cake. I looked down at my own cake. I wasn't hungry anymore.

Grandma and Grandpa were surprised we were calling again so soon. Daddy explained how he was going to have to leave before they got here. I listened to him talk while I traced the pattern of the material on my chair with my fingernail.

He finally handed the phone to me. "Not too long now," he said. "You're going to see them this weekend." I nodded.

"Hi," I said.

"How's my little Sarah Bernhardt?" Grandpa asked.

"Who?" I said.

"Never mind," Grandma said.

"She was a famous actress once upon a time," Grandpa said. "One of the best. Just like you. Are you all ready? When's the big premiere?"

"We do it for the elementary schools on Thursday and Friday. Then we have a performance for the parents on Friday night."

"We'll be there early Friday," Grandma said. "You know your Grandpa. By four o'clock Friday morning, he'll be telling me to get up so we can hit the road."

"That's right," Grandpa said. "It isn't every day our little girl has the lead in a play. Wild horses couldn't keep us away."

"I'm glad. I can't wait to see you."

"Where's that brother of yours?"

"He went to Nick's house to shoot baskets."

"Well, it sounds like he's making friends. That's nice," Grandpa said.

"I have to go now. Daddy said keep it short, so I'll see you in a few days."

"Okay, then. You take care," Grandpa said.

"And remember how much we love you," Grandma added.

I hung up the phone. My dad came back into the room. "They sound real anxious to see you again."

"Uh-huh."

He sat down in the chair next to me. "I'm sorry I won't be able to see the play. I know you've been working very hard."

"That's okay. You couldn't help it that you have to go out of town."

"Hey, I've got an idea! Why don't you ask Mrs. Johnson if I can come to the rehearsal tomorrow night. It might not be as good as seeing the play on Friday, but it would be the next best thing."

"Yeah, I'll ask her," I said. That made me feel better. Maybe he did want to see the play after all. I ran upstairs and got my stuff so Dad could take me to rehearsal. After we got finished, I asked Mrs. Johnson if it was okay for my dad to come to practice the next night. She said it would be just fine.

I came in the back door after school. Hattie was preparing fish fillets. She rolled the strips of fish in the batter and laid them on a cookie sheet. I sat on the cabinet and watched her.

"You're coming to see my play, aren't you, Hattie?"

"Wouldn't miss it for the world," she said. She got the oil out of the cabinet and poured it into the electric skillet. "I thought I'd make something real special on Friday night to celebrate your grandparents' visit and your opening night. What would you like?"

"Fried chicken!"

"How did I know that?" Hattie asked with a smile.

" 'Cause it's my favorite. With mashed potatoes and gravy and green beans," I told her.

Hattie laughed. "Okay, fried chicken it is." She lifted me off the counter. "Now go get cleaned up before your father gets home."

It turned out I had plenty of time to get cleaned up. The phone rang just before we sat down to dinner. It was my father. He was in a meeting, and it didn't look like he'd be home for dinner. I asked Hattie to let me talk to him.

"Dad? Aren't you coming to the play rehearsal tonight?"

"Oh, that's right. I completely forgot. I knew there was something I was supposed to do tonight, but it slipped my mind."

"Oh."

"I'll tell you what I'll do, I'll try to wrap this thing up as quickly as possible, and I'll meet you at the school."

"Okay."

We were late getting started because Mrs. Johnson had everyone try on their costumes. Mine was beautiful. It was a long pink dress with lace on it. I felt almost like a princess when I put it on. Anyway, it was almost eight o'clock by the time we started the play. My dad still wasn't there yet.

I kept watching for him to come in. We were using the stage lights. With those bright lights in your eyes, you can't see into the audience. I would see the door open every once in a while, and I tried to see if it was my dad, but I couldn't tell.

We finished the play, and Mrs. Johnson stood up and clapped for us. She had Jimmy bring up the house lights, and we all came out and sat on the edge of the stage for notes. Once the lights were up, I looked into the audience. There was no one there but the crew. I looked a second time, just to be sure. My dad wasn't there.

I wondered, If this had been one of Josh's football games, would he still have missed it? How was I ever going to show him I could do things if he never came to see me?

I went outside and saw Hattie waiting in the station wagon. I got in the front seat. "I'm sorry, peanut," she said. "He called right before I left the house. Said he wouldn't be home till late tonight. Sounded like he felt real bad about it."

"Sure."

"You know what I'm going to do? I'm going to take lots of pictures, and when he gets back from his trip, you can sit down and tell him all about it."

"Hattie, if he didn't come to the play, he sure isn't going to want to look at the pictures."

"Aw, peanut . . ."

"Let's just go home, Hattie."

"Sure." She started the car. I saw Mrs. Johnson coming out of the building carrying some of the costumes that needed to be altered. The whole time I was trying on my costume I was thinking how I couldn't wait to tell Hattie all about it. Now, none of it seemed to matter anymore. At least there had been one good thing that had come out of this play. I was going to get to see my grandparents. My dad might not care enough to leave his dumb old meeting for it. But they would drive halfway across Texas to be there for me. When I thought about that, I wondered why I was living with my dad.

11

I watched the clock slowly drag itself around to three-thirty. I thought the day would never end. I couldn't wait to get home. Grandma and Grandpa would be there. And even better, my dad wouldn't be.

I hadn't talked to my dad since he'd missed the rehearsal. Even though he came home late that night, I was still awake. I pretended to be asleep when I heard him open my door. He left early Wednesday morning without saying good-bye. He had left a note for us. He said he wished me luck in the play. He also said he was sorry about missing the dress rehearsal.

I ran in the back door that afternoon. Grandma and Grandpa were sitting at the kitchen table talking to Hattie. Hattie looked up and said, "Why, look who's here!" I wasn't sure if she meant me or my grandparents. I ran over to them and gave them the biggest hug I could.

"Well, how did the play go?"

"The little kids loved it, Grandpa. You should have seen them. They cheered and yelled. It was so much fun. Little kids are so funny."

"Well, you're not exactly an old lady, you know," Grandpa said.

I grabbed onto his hand. "Come on, I'll show you my room." They got up and followed me upstairs. I gave them a tour of the house. I showed them Josh's room and my room and the upstairs bathroom. Then I took them back downstairs and showed them my dad's room. "This is where you're going to sleep."

"Goodness, this place is so big, I'm surprised one of you kids hasn't gotten lost in here."

"Oh, Grandpa," I said.

We had Hattie's fried chicken for dinner just like she promised we would. It was almost as good as Grandma's. But I wouldn't tell either one of them that. They might feel bad. Even though dinner was really good, I was too excited to eat very much.

Hattie started clearing the table when we had finished. "Do we want dessert now or should we have it later when we get home?" she asked.

"Later," I voted. "I'm too nervous to eat it now. I might throw up."

"Well, I can have mine now," Grandpa said.

"You can wait, just like the rest of us," Grandma told him.

"There's plenty," Hattie said. "He can have some now and then he can have more when we get back tonight."

"Now there's a smart woman," Grandpa said.

"Hattie, you're going to spoil him. Here, I'll help you clear the table so we can get going."

"Don't bother, it's my job."

"Job or no job, I've been clearing tables since I was younger than Robin. I don't plan to start being waited on till I can't do it by myself anymore."

Hattie went over to cut Grandpa a piece of coconut cream pie. "Just a small piece now," Grandma said.

"Hush up, Gracie, and let the woman do her job," Grandpa said. He gave me a big wink. Hattie set the pie in front of him, and I ran off to get my things so we could leave.

The closer it got to seven-thirty, the more my stomach tied itself in knots. I had been a little nervous when we performed for the grade schools, but that was different. They were only little kids. If we had messed up, they probably wouldn't have noticed. But this time, there were parents in the audience. And even more important, my grandparents were here. I wanted to make them so proud.

* * *

106

When the curtain came down at the end, I knew we'd done good. I could just tell. We didn't make any mistakes at all. Well, there was one little mistake. When the guard stabbed Curdie, the hero, his ketchup pack splatted all over the stage and onto the guard. We had to run through ketchup the last part of the play. We were all laughing about it on the stage, but most people couldn't even see it from where they were sitting.

After the play was over, Mrs. Johnson had a hard time getting us to be quiet. We finally settled down. She took her glasses off and smiled at all of us. "I want to tell you how proud I am of each and every one of you. I feel so lucky to have a job that doesn't even feel like work. You've all tried so hard in the past month, and it shows. Don't make any plans after school on Monday because there's going to be an ice-cream sundae party in the theater room and all the ice cream you can eat."

We all cheered and Mrs. Johnson looked real happy. Laney got up and got the flowers we'd bought and the card we had all signed for Mrs. Johnson. Laney made a little speech about how much fun we'd had, and Mrs. Johnson cried. I looked at the new friends I'd made and was glad Laney had talked me into trying out for the play.

When we came out afterward, all of our parents were waiting for us. Grandpa hugged me and said,

"You were terrific! Didn't I tell you you were the next Sarah Bernhardt?"

"Who's Sarah Bernhardt?" Josh asked.

"Never mind," Grandma said. "You were wonderful, honey. We were so proud of you. I just can't get over how much you've grown in the last two months!"

"Do you really think so?" I asked hopefully.

"Naw," Josh said. "She hasn't grown much. You just forgot how big she was."

Hattie came up and put her arm on my shoulders. "Well, I think she's grown some. And I'm sure it's because of all my good cooking."

"Speaking of that, we'd better get on home. We've got some coconut cream pie waiting," Grandpa said.

"You already had yours," Grandma said.

"Well, I'm having some more."

Laney came up with her parents. I recognized her dad from that day at the club. He shook my hand. "Well, you are certainly a multi-talented young lady," he said. "A tennis pro and an actress."

"Well, I'm not sure I can do either as good as Laney yet."

"I wouldn't be too sure about that," her dad said.

Laney introduced me to her mother, and I introduced her to Hattie and my grandparents. Her dad shook hands with Grandpa. "Where's your father? I was looking forward to meeting him. Did he leave already?"

"Yeah, last Wednesday," I said.

"Huh?"

"He had to go to South America for a while."

"And miss the play? What a shame," Mr. Walker said. "I'll bet he felt terrible about that."

I wanted to say, "Don't be too sure." But instead I bit my tongue and said, "Sure."

I reminded Laney she was coming to dinner the next night and we all left. Hattie's coconut cream pie was just as good as it looked. And Grandpa said he liked the second piece even better than the first.

On Saturday, we went downtown and drove around Dallas. Hattie drove us because Grandma doesn't like to drive in the city, and Grandpa gets lost all the time. She took us to the West End for lunch. After lunch, we drove past the Kennedy Memorial.

Grandma and Grandpa got real quiet. Hattie parked the car, and we got out and walked down to the place where he was shot. Grandpa showed me the window in the textbook warehouse where Lee Harvey Oswald was supposed to have shot him from.

Grandpa put his arm around my shoulder. He

showed me the grassy knoll where they thought there had been a second gunman. It seemed strange that Grandpa had been alive then. I mean, it's something you read about in your history books, but you don't think about people you know actually being alive back then.

"The day it happened, I was just coming in from the barn. Grandma had been baking bread. She had flour on her cheek from where she'd touched her face. I knew the minute I walked in the door something real bad had happened."

Josh came over and stood beside us. Grandpa put his other arm around Josh. "Your grandma looked about ready to faint. She said, 'They've just shot the President.' It didn't register with me at first. Then I heard what the radio was saying, and I had to sit down."

"Did you cry when he died?" I asked.

Grandpa nodded. "Everybody did."

"Geez, Grandpa, how can you remember all this?" Josh asked.

"You know, it's funny, there are certain days you just can't forget. Now you ask me what I did a week ago Wednesday, and I probably can't even tell you what I had for breakfast. But you ask me what I was doing the day they bombed Pearl Harbor or the day they shot the President, and I can remember every detail. Right down to the flour smear on your grandma's face."

We all stood there for a minute and looked at the grassy knoll off in the distance. It was a funny feeling to be standing in the place where they'd shot the President. It made you feel real quiet and sad.

By the time we got back to my dad's house everyone was happy again. We were going to cook hamburgers out on the grill, and Laney was coming for dinner. I kept thinking Dallas wouldn't be a bad place to live if only Grandma and Grandpa lived there, too.

I didn't want to go to bed Sunday night because I knew that Grandma and Grandpa would be gone when I got up the next morning. I sat down on my Grandpa's lap. "Can't you stay a little longer?"

"Who would feed the stock? Edgar expects us back tomorrow. We've got to get home and tend to our chores."

"I wish I could go with you," I said sadly.

"And leave this pretty house and all your new friends? Now why would you want to do that?"

"Because I miss you," I said. I started to cry. Grandpa patted my head and held me close to him. I loved the way Grandpa smelled. His shirts smelled like the pipe tobacco he smoked after dinner. I thought about the nights we'd spent on the porch swing, and I wanted to climb into their trunk and hide so I could go back home with them.

Grandma took my hand and said, "Come on, I'll tuck you in." We went upstairs together. Back on the farm, Grandma used to come tuck us in every night. No one had tucked me in since I'd moved here. I don't think daddies know you're supposed to do that.

I brushed the hair off Grandma's forehead and touched her soft skin. I loved the way my grandma felt. She smiled at me. "I wish you didn't have to go," I told her.

"Well, you just think about how much fun you're going to have the rest of this year. And before you know it, it'll be summer, and you'll be coming out to spend a whole month with us."

Summer seemed a million years away. I wanted to go back with them now. I felt myself getting ready to cry again. I made myself stop before I started up. "Will you wake me up before you go tomorrow?"

"Oh, honey, it's going to be real early. I doubt the sun will even be up yet."

"I don't care. Please don't go without saying good-bye."

"All right, we'll wake you up when we leave."

"Promise?"

"Promise," she said. And just to be sure, she crossed her heart.

"I love you, Grandma," I said, sitting up and hugging her neck.

She wrapped her arms around me. "I love you, too, Robbie." She held me an extra-long time. I think it was because Grandma was the one who was ready to cry this time, and she didn't want me to know about it.

After she turned the light out and left, I got Harold out from under the covers. I thought how Grandma and Grandpa wouldn't be here tomorrow when I got ready for school, and that made me sad. Only this time I didn't try to stop the tears. I cried real hard, but Harold was the only one who noticed.

12

I sat on the counter the next afternoon and watched Hattie make supper even though I wasn't all that hungry. The ice-cream party after school had filled me up. I was telling Hattie all about it.

"I see," she said. "And just how many of these ice-cream sundaes did you eat, young lady?"

"About three."

"Three!"

"Well, I had to try all three kinds, didn't I? Besides, they were little ones."

Hattie reached over and pinched my stomach. It tickled and I laughed. "I can't believe you have room for all that in that little, bitty tummy of yours."

"Don't worry, I'll still try to make room for dinner."

"You bet you will. This is my famous noodle casserole. I only get to make this when your daddy's gone. He's not much for casseroles. But then, most men aren't."

Hattie took the noodles off the stove and drained the boiling water off of them. "You never know," she said. "Maybe by the time we're ready to eat, you'll have worked up a little appetite."

The back door opened. I looked up expecting to see Josh. I was surprised to see my dad walk in carrying his suitcase. So was Hattie. "Mr. W., what are you doing home so soon?"

"I got things wrapped up sooner than I expected." He set his suitcase down on the floor. He looked real tired. "Robin, what are you doing on the counter? I thought you weren't supposed to be up there."

I jumped off the counter and left the kitchen. I heard my dad say, "Is that what's going to happen every time Robin sees her grandparents?"

I stopped outside the door and listened. Hattie said, "Mr. Welborn, it's not her grandparents' doing."

"No? Then whose doing is it?"

"I guess it's mine."

"Mrs. Nelson, you and I seem to have different ideas about bringing up children. I think that's half the reason I haven't been able to get through to Robin."

"If you haven't been able to get through to her it's because you haven't been trying very hard," Hattie said.

"What does that mean?"

"Did you ever once ask her to play tennis with you? Have you taken an interest in anything she's done since she came to live with you? Do you have any idea how you broke that child's heart when you missed her play last week?"

"Mrs. Nelson, that couldn't be helped. It was business. I don't expect a child to understand a thing like that. But you're an adult. You should know there was nothing I could do about it. I have a job, and unfortunately that means I'm not always going to be available for every little thing."

"That play was *not* a little thing for Robin. Mr. Welborn, you have upset those children's lives by bringing them here. And I don't see you doing very much to make it any easier for them."

"Mrs. Nelson, I believe they're adjusting very well."

"That shows what you know. Josh may be doing all right. But Robin is lonely and unhappy and I can't just sit by and watch you break that little girl's heart anymore."

I wanted Hattie to be quiet before my father got really mad at her. I wanted to go into the kitchen and tell her that, but I was afraid. Then I knew by the sound of my father's voice it was too late for that anyway.

"That is quite enough," my father said. I had never heard him so angry.

"I suppose it is," Hattie answered.

"I think, Mrs. Nelson, you might be happier working somewhere else . . . for people you approve of."

"I guess you're probably right. But before I go, I want you to know that it's too bad you weren't here this weekend. Maybe if you'd seen how Robin is with her grandparents you wouldn't have been in such a hurry to take her away from them. Good day, Mr. Welborn."

I just couldn't stand there and let her go. I had to stop her. I ran into the kitchen. "Dad, please don't send Hattie away. I won't sit on the counter, anymore, I promise," I cried.

I wrapped my arms around Hattie's waist. "Please don't go. I love you."

Hattie took my arms in her hands and pulled them free. She patted my head and said, "I'm sorry, peanut. Your father is right. I don't belong in this house." She went into the laundry room and picked up her purse. I followed her to the back door and stood there crying while she got in her car and drove away.

I ran back into the kitchen. My father was standing near the sink. "You have to stop her. Tell her you didn't mean it," I pleaded.

"It's for the best, Robin. Believe me! We'll get a new housekeeper."

"I don't want a new housekeeper! I want Hattie," I cried.

"I'm sorry, Robin. It's not open for discussion."

"It wouldn't matter if it was. You never listen anyway! I hate you for this!" I screamed at him. "First you make me leave my grandma and grandpa, and now you make Hattie go away. I hate you!"

He grabbed my arm. "That's enough, Robin. You stop this at once!" I pulled away from him.

"I won't stop. I hate you. I hate you!" He shook me hard and told me to be quiet again. I was too mad to be quiet. I had been quiet since I came here, and now all my mad feelings were spilling out at once. "I wish you had died instead of Mommy."

That's when he slapped me. It surprised me more than it hurt me. No one had ever hit me before. My hand shot up to my face. We both stared at each other for a minute. Finally he said softly, "Go to your room."

I ran up the stairs and threw myself down on the bed and cried harder than I'd ever cried in my life. Eventually I fell asleep.

I heard someone knock on my door. It was Josh. He sat down on the bed beside me. "Dad told me Hattie left. He said you guys had a fight. I think he feels real sorry. Are you okay?"

"I hate it here, Josh."

"No, you don't. You're just mad at him right

now. Everything's going to be okay. You just wait and see."

I sat up and took hold of his arm. "Let's go home, Josh. You said we would, remember? You said if we didn't like it here, we could go home."

"Robbie, like I told you before, I like it here. I'm sorry if you're not happy, but I am." It didn't look like there was any more for us to say.

"Look, I brought you some dinner. Grandma always said you can't think on an empty stomach. You eat this and get a good night's sleep. We'll talk about everything in the morning. You'll feel a lot better. Just wait and see."

I looked at the casserole Hattie had been fixing earlier that afternoon. That afternoon seemed like a long time ago. I wondered what would have happened if I'd just jumped off the counter when I heard the back door open. Then Daddy wouldn't have gotten angry, and Hattie wouldn't have gotten fired, and everything would be okay.

I pushed the tray back toward Josh. "I'm not very hungry."

"I'll just leave it here. You might change your mind."

"I don't think so."

"I'll leave it anyway. Maybe Harold will want something to eat later tonight." Josh hugged me around the neck and rubbed his knuckles on the top of my head. "Cheer up, Robbie. Everything's going to work out." He went out and closed the door.

I got to thinking about what it had been like on the farm. Josh and I used to talk like that all the time. Since we'd come here, he was either with his friends or Dad. I had never felt so lonely.

I took Harold in my arms and rocked him back and forth. I kept remembering what Josh had said that morning on the farm when Dad came to get us. He had said if we didn't like Dallas, we would just get on a bus and go home. But Josh didn't want to go home anymore. This was his home now.

Then I realized there was nothing stopping me. I didn't need Josh. I could go home any time I wanted to. I wondered how much a bus ticket to Lubbock would cost. I knew where Hattie kept the kitchen money. It was in a cookbook in the pantry.

I looked at the tray Josh left. You know something? Hattie's casserole started to look very good. I ate my dinner, and I started making plans to leave. I would wait until my dad and Josh were in bed. Then I'd sneak down to the kitchen and see how much money was in the cookbook.

I was glad Josh brought the tray up. I would take it down with me. Just in case somebody woke up and wondered what I was doing in the kitchen.

I finished eating and got my suitcase out of the

closet. I started packing my clothes. I set Harold on the pillows to watch. I carefully packed the new dress Grandma had made me. I took some of the clothes my dad had bought, but not all of them. I didn't know if he'd want me to take them or not. I only took the ones I'd worn. After all, he couldn't take them back, and Josh or my dad couldn't wear them.

After I got everything packed I slid the suitcase off the bed and put it in the closet. I closed the door and tiptoed back to my bed. I took Harold in my arms and said, "We're going home, Harold." And I could tell he was real happy about it.

13

I left for school the next day, just like it was any other day. Only it wasn't like any other day. I didn't stay there. I left just before the first bell rang. I knew that even if the school called my house, no one would answer.

I went back to my house and got the phone book. I called Greyhound Bus Lines. I found out how much it would cost for a ticket to Wildflower, the town near my grandparents' farm. Then I got the bus schedule from Dallas to Wildflower. They had a bus that left at six-thirty. I felt very proud of myself for figuring all this out.

I counted the kitchen money again. There was sixty dollars. That would be enough money to get me to my grandparents and buy food along the way. I left a note for my dad and Josh telling them I was going to spend the night with Laney. *I will just ride to school with Laney in the morning*, I added on the note. That would give me plenty of time to get to Grandma and Grandpa's. Once I got home, I knew everything would be all right.

There was a bus stop on Preston Road, not far from my dad's house. I took my suitcase and Harold and went to the corner to wait for it. I tried to read the schedule that was posted there, but it was very confusing.

Fifteen minutes later a bus stopped in front of me. I asked the driver if he was going to the bus station. "Why that's clear downtown. You need to take this bus to Valley View Mall. Then take the downtown bus. It'll take you right to the bus station."

"Thank you," I said, putting my money into the slot. I picked up my suitcase and the bus driver stared at me.

"You aren't running away are you?"

"No," I said. I tried to give him my best smile. "I'm just going to visit my grandparents."

He smiled. "That's good. 'Cause I'd hate to be party to aiding and abetting a runaway."

"My dad's out of town, and the housekeeper's mother got sick so she had to leave, too. I'm going to my grandparents' to stay until he gets back."

He seemed to believe me. It was actually not all that hard to lie. I was kind of surprised about that. Normally I wasn't much good at lying.

It took me until lunchtime to get to the bus station. There was a Burger King right next door. That was probably a good thing because the bus station was in a real creepy part of Dallas. While I was there I think I saw the murderers and weirdos Grandma was worried about.

I bought my ticket and sat down to wait for my bus. I was glad I had Harold. At least I had something to hold onto. I wondered about all the people in the bus station. Some of them noticed me sitting there, and some of them acted like it was a normal thing to see an eleven-year-old kid sitting in the bus station waiting for a bus. Anyway, it was a very long afternoon.

The bus wasn't very crowded. I took a seat near the front and next to a window so I could see out. The man told me it would take about eleven hours to get to Wildflower. I guess that's 'cause buses have to go slower and they stop a lot.

I liked looking out the window. Dallas had a lot of pretty buildings. We went to Fort Worth and stopped there to pick up some people. There were still lots of seats. Most everyone had a seat all to themselves. A girl who was older than me got on the bus. She smiled at me and sat down across the aisle from me. Then the bus started up again.

The bus kept stopping and letting people on, and it was getting more crowded. A man got on and sat down next to the girl across from me. Every once in a while I would look over at him, and he would be staring at me.

I started to think about the stories I'd heard

about kids getting kidnapped and killed. What if that man wanted to kidnap me? No one would even know I'd been kidnapped for days because no one knew where I was going. My dad and Josh would think I was at Laney's, and my grandparents would think I was in Dallas, and I would be getting kidnapped by this strange-looking man on the way to my grandparents'.

I started getting really scared when it started getting dark out. I was thinking maybe this hadn't been such a good idea. I should have told Josh or Laney or somebody what I was doing in case I didn't show up. Most of the time when you run away you're supposed to leave a note. That way people know how to find you. I was wishing I'd left Josh a note.

The man across from me yawned loudly and stretched. I looked over at him. Did he have a gun in his belt? What if he was going to hijack the bus and make us go to Mexico or something? I didn't know how to speak Spanish. I wouldn't be able to tell anyone I had been kidnapped. I would never see my grandparents or Josh again. And I didn't have a passport. Even if I got away from him they might make me stay there! Running away was a dumb thing to do. I don't think I'd ever been more scared in my life.

We pulled into a bus stop. It was almost eleven o'clock. I wanted to go to the bathroom and get something to eat, but I was scared to get off the bus. I hadn't gotten up since we'd left Dallas. I just kept hoping if I sat back in the seat, no one would notice me. The strange man across the aisle got up to let the girl next to him out. He put his hand on the back of the seat next to me. I looked right into his eyes, and he smiled at me. I grabbed Harold and got up and followed the girl out of the bus.

They were frying hamburgers on the grill, and they smelled really good. I wanted something to eat, but I didn't want to lose track of the girl from the bus. I stayed where there were lots of people. What if the man had gotten off the bus after we did, and he was waiting for me to go off by myself so he could snatch me?

I looked over my shoulder, and I didn't see him anywhere. I was so busy looking back that I didn't see the girl from the bus stop in front of me. I ran right into her.

"I'm sorry," I said. She had dropped her purse and it spilled out all over the floor. I bent down to help her pick it up.

"You're from the bus, aren't you?" she asked. I nodded. "I saw you sitting across the aisle from me." She put the last of her things back into her purse and stood up. "I'm Sharon," she said, sticking her hand out to me.

I shook her hand, "My name's Robin."

"How far are you going?"

"I'm going to see my grandparents. They live just outside of Lubbock in a little place called Wildflower."

"Hey, I've heard of that. I go to school in Lubbock. At Texas Tech. I live in Fort Worth. My brother got married last weekend. I went home for the wedding."

She looked out the window. "I guess we'd better get back on the bus. It looks like we're getting ready to pull out." She looked at me. "Did you want to get something to eat? I'll wait for you."

I thought about those hamburgers again. I could see the people getting on the bus. I grabbed a bag of potato chips. "This is all I want," I said. We paid for our stuff and went back outside.

"You mind if I sit by you?" Sharon asked as we were climbing into the bus. "That guy next to me gives me the creeps."

"Sure," I said. For the first time since I'd gotten to the bus station that morning, I didn't feel so scared. I almost believed I was going to make it to my grandparents', and everything would be okay.

14

The strange man across the aisle didn't look so scary once we got back on the bus. I guess it was because Sharon was sitting next to me now, and I didn't feel so alone. She told me how she liked going to school in Lubbock. I told her about my grandparents' farm. And it didn't take long before we were both tired. There's just something about riding in a car or a bus that makes you sleepy. (And, of course, it was after midnight.)

I started dreaming about playing tennis. At first I was playing Laney. We were both dressed in those little white tennis outfits. Everything was moving in slow motion. I went after the ball. I caught it with a strong backhand. And when I looked up, Laney wasn't across from me anymore. My dad was standing on the other side of the net. He was dressed in white just like me.

I was so happy he wanted to play tennis with me. He was smiling and happy, too. He hit the ball and it sailed backward over my head. I turned to run after it, and I saw Josh standing behind me on the court. He yelled, "I got it!"

I watched the ball slowly sail back across the net. We were all moving like those football players on TV during the instant replay, when everything is in slow motion. My dad went for the ball, and I moved up to the net and waited for him to hit the next one to me.

It sailed over my head again. I went after it. Josh pushed me out of the way. I fell onto the asphalt, but neither of them noticed. They went on playing tennis as if I weren't there.

I got up and tried to break into the game. I was running all over the court trying to hit the ball. They were both laughing. I could hear Josh yelling, "Keep away! Keep away!" Pretty soon my dad was yelling it, too. I looked over at my dad and said, "I want to play, too."

He smiled at me and said, "Game's locked." They both started laughing. I sat down on the grass and cried.

I woke up, and I was still crying. It was almost two o'clock in the morning. I looked around the bus. Most of the people were asleep. Even the guy across the aisle had spread out across the seat and gone to sleep. I looked at Sharon. She was sleeping, too.

I clutched Harold to my chest and stared out the window. I hated waking up in the middle of the night after I'd had a scary dream. Usually, I would go into Josh's room and sleep in his bed. It was sad to think he wouldn't be in his room at Grandpa and Grandma's house this time. He would be back in Dallas with my dad.

I tried to reach way back in my mind and remember my dad from when I was a little girl. But I couldn't remember anything about him. I wondered if he loved me back then. Maybe he had only wanted Josh and not me, and that's why my parents had gotten a divorce. My mother had never talked about him much when she was alive. And my grandparents never said anything except when he'd send us something. Then they would say, "This is from your dad. He's in (wherever-he-was-at-that-time), now."

Until he came to get us three months before, that's all he was to me. A stranger who sent me presents at Christmastime and once in a while on my birthday.

Then one day we came home from school, and Grandma was looking very strange. I got scared. I thought maybe something had happened to Grandpa. But that wasn't it.

My father was moving back to the United States, and he had decided he wanted us to live with him. I said I wasn't going to do it. Josh did, too. Grandpa said that he *was* our father and anyway, if he refused he could just get a lawyer, and a judge would make us go live with him.

That scared me a little. What if my dad got a lawyer now and he took me back to live with him? I didn't think he would, though. Maybe if Josh and I had both left he would get a lawyer, but I didn't think he would get a lawyer just for me.

I thought about all the things that had happened since I'd gone to Dallas, from the first day when he forgot to come home and take my bike back like he promised, to his missing my play. It was pretty obvious to me that he wouldn't care very much if I was living there or not. I think it was my brother he wanted most. I guess that made me kind of sad. Anyway, I started to cry.

"Hey," Sharon said softly, "you okay?" I nodded. "Why don't I believe you?" She put her arm around me, and I leaned against her. "Why don't you tell me where you're really going?"

"To my grandparents," I said. "See, I used to live with them, and then my dad decided we should live with him, and he came and got my brother and me. Only I hated it there, so I'm going home. Because my daddy doesn't want me." Then I started to cry really hard.

Sharon didn't say anything at first. She just let me cry. Then she handed me a Kleenex out of her purse. "You know what happened to me when I was about your age? My parents got a divorce, and both of them got married to other people.

Then they had kids of their own, and I felt like I didn't belong anywhere."

"What'd you do?" I asked.

"I spent a lot of time being angry and thinking about how sorry they would be if I ran away."

"Did you do it?"

"Nope. One day I started thinking how lucky I was to have two families of my very own. I liked my new little brothers and sisters. And I guess I liked my step-parents most of the time. Now when I go home, I stay with both my families. And I get twice as many presents at Christmas and two parties on my birthday. And there are twice as many people to love me."

"But that's just it. My dad doesn't love me."

"I bet he does."

"No, he doesn't. He only likes my brother."

"I'm sure that's not true."

"But he's always doing things with my brother. And he never has time for me."

"Maybe it's easier for him to relate to a boy. He might not have had much experience with a girl. He might not know what he should do with you. You might have to tell him."

"Was that what you had to do?"

"I didn't really know my dad at all until my parents got divorced. Then he started spending a lot of time with my brother and me. At first, I felt like we didn't have anything in common. Then we found our own special things, and now I see that my dad loves me just as much as he loves my brother. It's just that he shows it in different ways. I'll bet you anything, your dad loves you, too. And he's probably pretty worried right now."

Sharon looked at her watch. "It's almost three o'clock. We'd better get some sleep. We'll get into Lubbock in a couple of hours. I've got an eight o'clock class I'll probably sleep through, as it is."

"Okay."

Sharon looked at me. "You going to be all right?"

"Sure."

"Think about what I said. Sleep on it. Maybe you'll be getting a bus ticket back to Dallas in the morning. I'll bet your dad would be glad to see you."

I settled back into my seat and wondered about that. I didn't think so. I think he would just be glad I was gone, and he wouldn't have to remind me not to sit on the kitchen counter anymore or to stop doing things that weren't ladylike. If he was glad for anything, it would be that I'd left.

15

The sun was coming up just as we pulled into Lubbock. I looked over at Sharon. She was still asleep. When the bus stopped, she woke up.

She started gathering her stuff. "Well, I guess this is it," she said. "You going to be all right?" She looked at the man across the aisle from us who was still sleeping. I nodded.

"Think about what I told you," she said. "I'm sure your dad is worried sick right now." She leaned down and hugged me. She put a piece of paper in my hand. "My name and phone number in case you get into trouble. Call me and let me know how this works out."

"Thanks. I will." The bus driver announced they were getting ready to pull out. Sharon quickly made her way off the bus. I waved to her out the window as we drove away.

It was another hour to Wildflower. We stopped in front of the cafe and post office. I got Harold and stood up. I accidently hit the man's feet who was sleeping across from me. He woke up and looked out from under his hat. "Getting off here?" he said.

I shrugged my shoulders. "Maybe." I mean, what if he got off, too, just to follow me?

"Well, good luck, kid," he said. He settled back against the window and put his hat down over his face again. I hurried off the bus.

The bus driver had set my suitcase on the sidewalk. When I picked it up he asked, "Isn't someone here to meet you?"

"My grandparents are coming. They're probably late. I'll just sit here and wait." I carried my suitcase back to the bench outside the post office and sat down to show him I really meant it.

He got back on the bus and drove away. As soon as he was out of sight, I got up and went into the cafe. I was going to have to walk to my grandparents' farm. It was about five miles, but I didn't have much choice. I was going to leave my suitcase inside the cafe, and come back for it later. There was no way I could walk five miles carrying my suitcase.

Opal was behind the counter in the cafe. Breakfast sure smelled good. I didn't have enough time or money to get anything, though.

Opal looked up from the counter she was wiping down and saw me. "Why, Robbie Welborn, what are you doing in these parts? Your grandpa told me you'd gone off to live in Dallas."

"Well, I'm back," I said. "Hey, Opal, can I leave this suitcase here till later?"

"Sure. Are your grandparents coming to get you?"

"Well, it's kind of a surprise. They don't actually know I'm coming."

She nodded her head thoughtfully. "I see. Sort of a surprise visit."

"Yeah. So anyway, can I leave this here?"

"Sure." I took it around to the side of the counter, and Opal lifted it easily. She put it under the counter and scooted it in tight with her foot. "No one will ever know it's there till you come back for it."

"Thanks." I went out the door and started down the road to my grandparents' farm. After the first mile I was thinking this was the second stupid thing I'd done. It takes a lot longer to walk five miles than you think it does.

I heard honking from behind me, and I jumped to the side of the road. My heart was pounding so hard I was afraid it was going to pop out of my shirt. I was scared to look back and see who was coming. What if that weirdo had gotten off the bus and come after me? At least Opal and Sharon knew where I was going now.

Henry pulled up in the mail truck. He slid his window open and leaned out. "What're you doing walking on this road so early in the morning?" he asked.

"I'm going home."

"How about a lift?"

"I'd love it," I said gratefully. I climbed inside the crowded mail truck and found a place to sit down.

"Your grandpa didn't say nothing about you coming for a visit when we played billiards the other day."

"I'm kind of surprising them," I said.

"I see. Running away, huh?"

"Well, not exactly. Right now, I guess I'm just visiting for a while."

Henry kept chattering away about how he liked this time of year the best because he felt just right. He said the heat nearly killed him in the summer, and he didn't have any air-conditioning in the truck. Then he said how the cold in the winter gives him rheumatism 'cause the heater doesn't work worth a darn. Me, I was just glad to be riding. I wouldn't have cared if it was on a donkey.

Henry pulled the truck to a stop at my grandparents' mailbox. "Here, you may as well take them the mail as long as you're headed that way."

"Thanks for the ride, Henry," I said, taking the few letters he'd handed me and climbing down out of his truck.

"Oops. Don't forget this. Your grandpa will have my hide if he doesn't get his morning paper." He handed me a rolled newspaper through the window and drove away.

I walked up the dusty road toward the house. Grandpa was just coming out of the barn with the milk pail when I got to the fence. He set the pail down so hard some of it splattered out on the ground. Then he stood there staring at me for a few minutes like he thought he might be dreaming.

"Hi, Grandpa," I said, just to show him I was real.

"Robbie? What on earth are you doing here? Did your daddy send you? Where's Josh?"

"It's just me, Grandpa. I didn't like Dallas very much. So I came home."

"Well, come on inside. You're just in time for breakfast." I ran up beside him, and he put his arm on my shoulders and walked me into the house. "Grandma, we got company for breakfast."

Grandma came into the kitchen and almost dropped to the floor. "Robin, what are you doing here?"

"I'm coming home," I said.

16

Grandma set breakfast down and it tasted as good as Opal's breakfast had smelled back at the cafe. "So how did you get here?" Grandma asked me.

"On a bus."

"Where's your suitcase?"

"I left it at the cafe. It was too heavy to carry. I walked the first mile. Then Henry gave me a ride."

"Does your daddy have any idea you're here?" she asked. I shook my head. Grandma got up and went to the phone. "He must be worried sick."

"He thinks I'm at Laney's. Even if he knew, I don't think he'd care that much."

Grandma came back over and sat down. She took my hand in hers. "Now, why would you say a thing like that?"

I started to cry. "He never cares about anything I do. I try really hard, but it doesn't matter. He likes everything Josh does. He never misses his football games. He even watches Josh do his goofy dives off the high board at the club."

I sniffed a few times, and Grandma handed me one of the Kleenexes she always keeps stuffed in her sleeves. I wiped my nose. "I tried to like it there. Honest. But I don't. I want to stay here. I don't think Daddy will care. As long as he has Josh, it won't matter if I'm there or not."

Grandma put her arms around me. "Oh, honey. I'm sure he cares. We have to call him and let him know you're all right. Then we'll decide what to do about all this."

"There's nothing to decide. I don't want to go back. If you make me go back, I'll just run away again."

Grandma got up and dialed the phone. Grandpa patted the top of my arm with his rough old hand. My heart started racing when I heard my grandma say, "Hello, Willis. I believe you may be missing something, and we have her here."

I almost threw up my breakfast. I was wishing I hadn't eaten so much. "Just relax," Grandpa said softly. "No one's gonna make you go back if you don't want to."

Grandma hung up the phone. "He's going to get the first flig   t here. He'll call and let us know when to expe   him."

Grandma pushed my hair off my face with her cool hand. "Why don't you go get some rest? I doubt you slept much on a bus. You look like you're about ready to drop."

"I'll go on into town and get your suitcase," Grandpa said.

"Just be sure you leave your pool cue in the truck," Grandma said. "I want you back here before lunchtime."

"You're a slave driver, old woman," he said. Then he kissed both of us good-bye.

I laid on my old quilt and pulled on the strings till I fell asleep. When I woke up, I thought I was dreaming. The sun was coming through the window and falling across my bed. Harold was sleeping on the pillow beside me. I looked around the room and realized this wasn't a dream. I was back in my old room. I was home.

I went downstairs. Grandma was rolling out a piecrust. I hopped up on the counter to watch. "Can I make a crispy?" I asked.

"Get down off there, young lady," Grandma scolded. "You know better than that." I jumped off the counter. She handed me a little ball of dough. "Here. Make a crispy."

I ran over to the breadboard and rolled the dough out just the way I like it. Grandma handed me the cinnamon and sugar. I sprinkled them on the dough and put it on a cookie sheet. Then I put it in the oven.

"Your daddy will be here about three o'clock," Grandma said. I looked at the clock on the kitchen wall. It was almost noon. Grandpa came in the back door. "Something smells mighty good in here."

"Get washed up. It's almost time for lunch," Grandma said.

"We having apple pie for dessert?" Grandpa asked.

"No. We'll have that this afternoon. When Willis gets here."

"You can have some of my crispy, Grandpa," I said.

I watched TV all afternoon. It felt funny to be home watching TV when I should be in school, and I wasn't sick or anything. I wondered what Laney was doing today. I wondered what Mrs. Johnson would think when I didn't come back to school.

I heard car tires scrunching on the gravel road outside, and I knew my dad was here. The butterflies in my stomach were dancing around again. I wanted to run up to my room and hide. Instead, I squeezed myself down into the chair as small as I could and hoped he wouldn't see me.

I heard him knock on the kitchen door, and then Grandma said, "Come on in. She's in the living room watching TV."

I stared at the TV and looked straight ahead.

He kneeled beside the chair. "We missed you last night," he said. He put his hand on my knee. "I'm glad you're safe. I was worried sick when your grandmother told me what you'd done."

I looked at the TV. Why was he being so nice now? He wasn't nice before, when he fired Hattie or when he hit me. He was probably just being nice so my grandparents wouldn't see what he was really like and take Josh away, too.

"Robin, I'm sorry about the fight we had the other night. I was just so tired. I wasn't thinking very clearly. And I'm really sorry I slapped you. I feel so terrible. I was going to talk to you, but I wanted to wait until last night when we were both calmer. I was afraid I'd say the wrong things otherwise. What I wanted to say is that I wish you'd give me another chance." He sounded like he was going to cry. "Come home with me, Robin."

"I am home."

Grandma put her hand on the back of my chair. "Robbie, why don't you run on to your room and let us talk to your daddy for a while?"

I got up and went to my room without another word. I picked up Harold off my pillow and slid back into the corner on my bed. I played with the strings on my quilt.

Why was he being so nice all of a sudden? He had what he wanted, didn't he? He had Josh all to himself. That's probably what he really wanted all along. Only he couldn't just take Josh and leave me here. Josh wouldn't have gone. I knew he wouldn't. So my father got stuck with both of us. Sort of a package deal. You know, buy one, get one free.

Someone knocked on my door. "Come in," I said.

My dad came in and sat on the edge of my bed. It reminded me of times Josh used to do that. In fact, he kind of looked like a grown-up version of Josh sitting there in my room.

"Your grandparents told me you don't want to go back to Dallas." I looked down at Harold and started to pull on the fur around his ear. "I know it's hard for you to believe, but I'll miss you very much. I've sort of gotten used to having a little girl around my house. It's going to seem very lonely without you."

He reached down and pulled the strings of the bedspread. "I'm not going back until tomorrow. Maybe you could show me around the farm later?"

"Okay. Who's taking care of Josh?" I asked.

"Oh, didn't I tell you? Mrs. Nelson's back."

"Hattie's back?"

"Yes, Hattie's back. I called to apologize to her, and when I asked her to give us a second chance she said she would." He took my hand. "I wish you'd give me a second chance, too. Mrs. Nelson may have made me angry, but she may have been right about a few things, too. I guess the only time we really connected was that night we went out to dinner. Sometimes I think about that, and wonder why it can't be like that all the time. Maybe I'm not used to kids. With Josh, it was easier. You know, his being a boy and everything."

He got off the bed and held his hand out to me. "How about that tour now?" I took his hand.

I walked him down to the swimming hole and showed him the fort Josh and I had built in a gully in the hills. I showed him everything about the farm. He held my hand the whole time.

"I'd forgotten how beautiful this old farm was."

"You've been here before?"

"Years ago. With your mother. I grew up on military bases all over the world. I'd never even been on a farm until I met your mother."

"I didn't know that," I said.

"There's a lot we have to learn about each other."

We walked up onto the porch and sat down on the old swing. Just like me and Grandpa always do. Daddy put his arm around my shoulders. "I want you to know that I don't blame you for wanting to come back here. But I am going to miss you. I hope you'll come visit us a lot."

"I will," I told him.

"And maybe one of these days you'll change your mind and want to come live with me again. Of course, you may have to help me out some. I haven't had much experience with having a daughter. Even us big guys make mistakes, you know."

We rocked back and forth with no noise but the squeaking of the old porch swing. I was starting to understand why Josh and my dad got along so well. In a lot of ways, Josh and my dad were kind of alike. Sitting there, talking to him, it was almost like being out on the porch with my brother.

I liked my dad when he was like he was that afternoon and the night he'd taken me out to dinner. But I couldn't help thinking, What would happen if I went back with him? Would things be better? Or would they just go on like they had before?

17

My dad came into the kitchen the next morning. He was trying to button the sleeves of his shirt. "Here, let me get that," Grandma said.

"I'll do it," I said, stepping in front of her. "That's my job."

"Yes, but who'll do it for me now that you're living here? I'll have to go around with my sleeves flapping all day." He smiled at me. It made my heart feel sad.

After breakfast, I watched my dad drive away in the rental car. He had promised to send the rest of my things up next week. It looked like I was home to stay. But it didn't feel as good as I had thought it would.

Grandpa said I would have to get enrolled in school again. I hadn't thought much about school. They didn't even have theater classes for my grade. And where was I going to play tennis? I didn't know anybody in Wildflower with a tennis court. I sat on the porch swing long after the dust had settled in the road from my dad's car.

In fact, I sat on the porch swing a lot the next couple of days. I didn't remember ever being so lonely here before. I missed Josh a lot. Even if we were doing our own things in Dallas, at least I got to see him sometimes. Now it might be weeks before I saw him again.

Grandpa came out of the barn and climbed the steps of the porch. He sat down beside me. "Nice day, huh?"

"Yeah."

"Wonder what the weather's like in Dallas today?"

"I don't know."

"I wonder that a lot lately. Wonder if you're getting rained on when it's raining here or if you're swimming in that pool over to the country club when it gets real hot."

"I think about you a lot, too," I said.

"Wonder what your daddy's thinking right now?"

"I don't know."

"Maybe we ought to give him a call tomorrow morning and see how they're getting along without you."

"Maybe."

"Yeah, well, I reckon your grandma's probably got supper on the table. We better get on in 'fore she throws it out."

I couldn't figure it out. The whole time I was in Dallas, all I wanted was to come home. Now I was home, and all I kept thinking about was what they were doing in Dallas.

The next morning, my grandpa dialed my dad's number and I started to get scared. What if he didn't want to talk to me? What if he didn't mean any of the things he had said the other day, and he was just trying to be nice? Grandpa handed me the receiver. My hand was shaking. "What will I say?" I asked.

"Don't worry about it. He's your daddy. You'll think of something."

Josh answered the phone. He sounded terrific. I think he was happy we'd called. "Hattie's back," Josh said.

"I know. Dad told me."

"When are you coming back, Robbie? It's crazy here. I get to watch whatever I want on TV, and I hate it. Sometimes I go in your room to see if maybe you came back while I was gone. I miss you. Everybody does."

"I miss you, too."

"Well, here's Dad. He wants to talk to you. He's about to tear the phone out of my hand."

"Did I hear Josh say you're ready to come home?" he asked. I looked at my grandparents. I loved them so much. Could I really leave them again? Then I thought about what Sharon had said on the bus the other day. About having two families. I thought about my grandparents. Then I thought about Josh and my dad and Hattie back in Dallas. And I knew I had two families to love, too.

"Yeah, I'm ready to come home," I said.

I stayed at my grandparents' house till Sunday afternoon. We drove over to Lubbock so I could get on the plane to fly home. I was real glad about that. I didn't want to take the bus again. One bus trip is enough to last anybody for a while.

When we got to the airport, I asked Grandpa if I could make a call. I took Sharon's phone number out of my pocket. The phone rang a long time. I was about to hang up when I heard her pick up the receiver.

"Sharon? It's Robin. You know, from the bus?"

"Sure, Robin. I remember you. What's up? Are you in trouble or anything?"

"No, everything's great. I just called to tell you you were right. I'm going home."

Sharon seemed real glad that everything had worked out. She said she would call me when she came home from school next summer, and we would go to the movies or something.

This time when I got on the plane, Grandma and Grandpa looked happy. They were both smiling and waving. And I didn't feel so scared about having to leave them this time.

Before leaving for the airport, Grandpa had come into my room. He sat on my bed and picked up Harold. "You and this bear go back a long ways," he said. "I bought him for you at the airport the day your mama brought you here from South America. You were just a little bitty girl."

"I remember," I said.

"Robbie, you just remember, you've always got a home here with us if things don't work out in Dallas." He sat Harold back down on the bed and held his arms out to me. I went to him, and he hugged me so tight I almost couldn't breathe. "We love you."

I got off the plane and saw my dad standing with all the other people at the gate. He was easy to spot. He was waving a big teddy bear in the air.

He grabbed me and hugged me as tight as Grandpa had that morning. "I'm glad you decided to give Dallas a second chance," he said.

"Where's Josh?"

"He's helping Hattie fry up a chicken so we can all celebrate together."

"Oh, I almost forgot." He handed me the bear. "This is for you. That poor old bear you drag around looks like he's seen better days."

I looked down at Harold. He *had* seen better days. But he'd seen worse ones, too. I realized my dad and I really *did* have a lot to learn about each other. Harold wasn't just a bear. He was . . . well, he was Harold. And there was only one Harold. But I'd keep the other bear anyway. Living in Dallas kept me pretty busy. Harold might need a friend.

I waited for my dad to get my suitcase at the baggage claim, and thought about what my grandpa had said to me. I could always go back to Lubbock if this didn't work out. But I had a feeling both of us were going to try a lot harder this time.

A man bumped into the huge bear my dad had bought me and almost knocked him out of my arm. "Oops, sorry. Hey, that's some bear," he said.

"Yeah, my dad bought him for me."

"He must be quite a dad. You're one lucky little girl," he said.

I looked at my dad making his way through the people carrying my suitcase and answered, "Yeah, I sure am."

I had two houses and two families and both of them wanted me. I think just knowing I could go back to my grandparents' anytime I wanted to made me feel a lot safer. I wasn't sure things were going to work out with my dad this time, but I was sure I was going to give it a better chance than I had the first time.

My dad put his arm around me and said, "You ready to go home?"

"Yep," I answered. And I really was.

APPLE*PAPERBACKS

Pick an Apple and Polish Off Some Great Reading!

NEW APPLE TITLES

☐	MT43356-3	Family Picture Dean Hughes	**$2.75**
☐	MT41682-0	Dear Dad, Love Laurie Susan Beth Pfeffer	**$2.75**
☐	MT41529-8	My Sister, the Creep	
		Candice F. Ransom	**$2.75**

BESTSELLING APPLE TITLES

☐	MT42709-1	Christina's Ghost Betty Ren Wright	**$2.75**
☐	MT43461-6	The Dollhouse Murders Betty Ren Wright	**$2.75**
☐	MT42319-3	The Friendship Pact Susan Beth Pfeffer	**$2.75**
☐	MT43444-6	Ghosts Beneath Our Feet Betty Ren Wright	**$2.75**
☐	MT40605-1	Help! I'm a Prisoner in the Library Eth Clifford	**$2.50**
☐	MT42193-X	Leah's Song Eth Clifford	**$2.50**
☐	MT43618-X	Me and Katie (The Pest) Ann M. Martin	**$2.75**
☐	MT42883-7	Sixth Grade Can Really Kill You Barthe DeClements	**$2.75**
☐	MT40409-1	Sixth Grade Secrets Louis Sachar	**$2.75**
☐	MT42882-9	Sixth Grade Sleepover Eve Bunting	**$2.75**
☐	MT41732-0	Too Many Murphys	
		Colleen O'Shaughnessy McKenna	**$2.75**
☐	MT41118-7	Tough-Luck Karen Johanna Hurwitz	**$2.50**
☐	MT42326-6	Veronica the Show-off Nancy K. Robinson	**$2.75**

Available wherever you buy books...or use the coupon below.